FINDING MARCO

Kenneth C. Cancellara

Synergy Books

Finding Marco
Published by Synergy Books
P.O. Box 30071
Austin, Texas 78755

For more information about our books, please write us, e-mail us at
info@synergybooks.net, or visit our web site at www.synergybooks.net.

Publisher's Cataloging-in-Publication available upon request.

LCCN: 2010922171

ISBN-13: 978-0-9842358-6-5
ISBN-10: 0-9842358-6-8

10 9 8 7 6 5 4 3 2 1

Life's voyage
And its final destination
Predestined.
But its meanderings not
Predetermined.
Youthful green shoots
Foretell traits
With detours and
Adventures
Along its path

PROLOGUE

As a six-year-old boy, Marco Gentile was already a seasoned athlete—a cross-country runner, to be precise. In the small town of Acerenza, Italy, where he lived, the school hours were 8:00 a.m. to 1:00 p.m., with no breaks for playtime. Acerenza sits on a hilltop in the Southern Apennines—that string of mountain ranges that, like a spinal cord, extends from the northern plains of Lombardy through central southern Italy to the provinces of Basilicata and the northern part of Calabria.

Within five minutes of the school teacher ringing the dismissal bell, Marco would neatly fold his school uniform jacket and put it in his backpack, and begin his daily five-mile run from the town-center—passing through the Gate of San Canio and following the winding country paths down the mountain—to Alvanello, the family vineyard and farm deep in the valley. These paths had been created not by engineers or architects, but by Acerenzesi and their mules and donkeys. For innumerable years, the townspeople and their animals pounded the earth twice a day: at dawn, traveling down the mountain to their farms, and late in the evening, traveling back up to their homes in town. With the passage of time, the earth underfoot had become so hardened by the constant use that it was as slick as asphalt. Still, the haphazard meanderings of these paths around large rocks, trees, and crevices, and their twists and turns around the steep mountain, created a dangerous voyage for the inattentive.

But not for Marco. Marco knew every bit of topography, every roll, steep or gentle, by heart. He knew the placement of every protruding tree root or rock, and never needed to slow his pace to avoid them. Down the mountain he would run at reckless speed, aided by gravity and his precocious athletic fitness. He confidently gained pace at the very places where other, less formidable pedestrians would need to slow down.

As Marco got closer to his destination, he would nervously gaze at the other side of the valley toward the railway station to confirm that his daily race opponent—the train arriving from Potenza at precisely 2:00 p.m.—had not yet pulled in. When Marco heard the screeching of steel wheels against railway tracks, he knew that the train had turned into the last tunnel before its straightaway into the station. This was a signal for Marco to dig deep for more energy to begin his own final sprint to the farmhouse finish line.

Most times, Marco would land in his grandfather's waiting arms seconds before the whistle announcing the arrival of the train reverberated in the valley.

"Well done, Marco," his grandfather would say approvingly. With a proud smile, he would pat his grandson's back and solemnly declare, "Soon, we will have to find a more worthy opponent for you." Those precious words of approbation from his grandfather were all the reward Marco sought for his daily challenge. His own inner sense of pride in having succeeded in achieving his goal was sufficient; there was no need for external rewards.

It seemed that, at a very young age, Marco had developed an innate ambition to succeed—a drive to win that would serve him well in his future career.

PART I

With the passage from youth,
Idealism succumbs to
Ambition and rewards.
The hunger to succeed
And find tenure
Become life's guiding passions.
The strong strive,
The weak cower.
Until the internal odyssey
Begins.

CHAPTER 1

As a young university student in Toronto, Canada, Mark Gentile had craved little else than to be an advocate and to employ his oratorical skills to sway a judge or a jury. His ambition, in his early years as a prosecutor, was raw and single-minded. He wanted to win, perhaps even at all costs. There were times when he himself had had a faint doubt as to an accused person's culpability. But one of Mark's best characteristics was tenacity, and so he persevered in each case, prioritizing evidence, preparing witnesses flawlessly, and weaving in just the right amount of advocacy with evidentiary facts and legal doctrines to secure convictions.

Within a couple of years of the start of his legal career at the Department of Justice, he had already become a feared adversary of even the most seasoned defense counsel. Although every opponent who faced Mark in court knew he was in for a battle, Mark's reputation was one of principled fairness toward his colleagues at the bar, the judiciary, and the adversarial, often hostile, witnesses he faced.

This is exactly how Mark Gentile wanted to be known, as a fair and tough prosecutor. He was as amenable to settling matters outside the legal process as he was to take cases to full and aggressive trials—and even to appeals where circumstances warranted.

At the start of his legal career, Mark had wanted only to be an advocate—a "barrister" in the traditional English characterization. He'd had no premonition of the twists and turns that awaited him, both inside and outside the practice of law.

After four years of "battling in the trenches," as Mark termed it, he knew that an important decision needed to be made. Should he stay with the Department of Justice permanently or move on to employ his acquired legal skills in private practice? This was not a decision Mark took lightly. He had very much enjoyed his last four years with the government and the power he felt whenever he needed to flash his Department of Justice identity card; the belief that he always acted for "the good guy" in every case he prosecuted; and the conviction that what he did wasn't just professionally fulfilling on a personal level, but that it made a real difference to the society of which he was a part. He consistently looked forward to the adrenaline rush he felt at the beginning of every court appearance, and the delicious laziness that came from being drained of energy upon the announcement of every verdict.

He compared trials to running a marathon: the painful days of physical exhaustion and mental suffering in training for the race; the anxiety spells and butterflies just before the start of the race; the exhaustion midway through the race; the second wind picked up inexplicably just as the physical and mental batteries were being drained; and finally, the euphoric climax of crossing the finish line, exalted by having successfully challenged physical and mental limitations. And so it was for his court work. For each trial, there was the exhausting preparation, followed by the exhilarations and disappointments encountered during the course of the trial, and invariably the end accompanied by a full energy depletion, as if someone had clicked the off button. But just as invariably, after a brief pause to allow his body to restore itself, Mark would again be ready to commence the same training regimen for his next court appearance. The course for the next case would be different, but the preparations; the surges of adrenaline;

and the personal, physical, emotional, and mental experiences would remain unchanged. The challenge, the discipline, and the unpredictability were the reasons why Mark lived for the big race—whether in court or on the pavement.

Indeed, it had been a life he had found satisfying and enjoyable to this point, but Mark Gentile knew that his legal learning curve had just about reached its peak. If he wanted to progress into other, as yet uncharted, waters, he needed to make a move now, while he was still young enough to be an attractive target to potential employers and still flexible enough to venture into untapped legal fields. He had practiced exclusively in the criminal field for over four years, and while he had achieved a level of comfort in that particular discipline, he felt that it was time to venture into other areas of the law.

Curtin & Joseph LLP was a reputable and renowned national law firm with offices in major cities from coast to coast. Established over one hundred years ago, the firm had grown considerably, both in size and prestige, over the years. Curtin & Joseph had a large and well-respected litigation department, but it was known principally as a legal powerhouse in the corporate-commercial area. The firm's clients included some of the largest and best-known corporations, especially in the energy field.

Mark was attracted to Curtin & Joseph precisely because a position there would provide him an entry into the legal world of big business. At the firm, he would have the opportunity to interact with sophisticated and professional executives and litigate issues that were material to their corporate success, which excited him. The more Mark considered the prospect of working in Curtin & Joseph's Toronto office, the more he became convinced that he wanted to focus on big business. He hoped it could be where he left his mark. Learning of his interest in their firm, Curtin & Joseph was delighted to have attracted a young and talented man like Mark Gentile. His considerable reputation as a criminal trial lawyer had permeated the entire legal profession; it was an accepted fact that he was an up-and-comer. All Curtin & Joseph needed to do was convert Mark's experience, expertise, and passion as a litigation counsel from the "dungeon" (as the criminal courts were often called) to the civility of litigating merger and acquisition issues, matters involving oppression remedies and contracts—in short, legal issues that concerned dollars rather than life and liberty.

Mark gave his notice at the Department of Justice, and soon signed on as a partner at Curtin & Joseph. Mark felt more than ready for the new job. He began working tirelessly to defend the interests of his new firm's corporate clients. Mark's tenacity, considerable work habits, and skills of articulation endeared him to the senior corporate executives for whom he acted and with whom he mingled.

Mark found his switch into civil law seamless and painless, and within a short time, his reputation as a business litigator had grown to the point that some of the largest corporations sought him out as their advocate. Indeed, Mark had so quickly grown in stature that certain clients attempted to dangle retainers in front of him and his firm in order to prevent him from representing their competitors in the future. The conflicts committee of Curtin & Joseph was kept busy determining whether retainers for Mark's services ought to be accepted or rejected—a determination that would be made only after careful scrutiny of the nature and value of the proposed retainers. They principally analyzed whether the retainer was sought to advance or defend current issues, or whether it was merely a ploy to prevent Mark from being legitimately retained in the future to accept an opposing brief.

Mark Gentile's practice was thriving. Not only did he litigate some of the most important corporate and commercial issues arising in the world of business, he also advised boards of directors and senior executives on strategic issues that had little to do with litigation per se. The latter retainers were the most satisfying to Mark because they indicated that he had achieved a high level of maturity and business acumen; he now had the trust of the top decision makers. As a result, Mark's interest in law switched—gradually at first, but later with increasing velocity—from that of pure litigation to that of business advising. He became more interested in participating in corporate strategies in the boardroom, than in litigating in the courtroom.

Even as a lawyer, Mark showed a special aptitude for business decision making, and an understanding of the importance of legal ethics. And while there was little opportunity to exercise his entrepreneurial talents in his daily practice of law, he taught an ethics course at his alma mater to third-year law students, as they embarked on the mixed trajectory of pursuing a profession that was honorable and, at the same time, like any other profession, needed to show a profit. Mark felt a sense of accomplishment and personal pride in playing a small role in guiding young minds in their career paths.

But Mark was ready for much bigger challenges. He had developed an insatiable appetite for corporate business, and he was ready for a new chapter in his career.

CHAPTER 2

Of all the clients whom Mark served at Curtin & Joseph, none was as charismatic, progressive, passionate, and eccentric as seventy-year-old Gordon Welsh. Mark and Gordon became close friends almost from the start. Gordon had been a client of Curtin & Joseph since his early days as an individual investor in a newly created public offering. Gordon had a sixth sense for investing in successful start-ups and he became somewhat of a legend at Curtis & Joseph, not only for his meticulous financial analyses, but also for his innate sense of fair dealing.

Mark had initially been introduced to Gordon to provide corporate governance advice to him and to his board of directors. Soon, the two had struck a tight relationship and Mark became Gordon's "go-to" attorney whenever he sought legal advice. Gordon's trust in Mark grew to the point that Mark became Gordon's sounding board even on non-legalistic business decisions.

Two decades earlier, Gordon had become a media darling when he had announced that he was starting up a new North American automobile manufacturer to compete head-on with Detroit's "Big Three" and with the European and Asian auto industries. But he wouldn't be just another carmaker. Gordon's idea was simple and yet tantalizingly eloquent: build small cars that saved energy and were environmentally friendly. Gordon's dream had been announced at a time when neither the environment nor energy consumption were relevant issues among the majority of the world's population. In those days, fossil energy depletion had not been often thought about, much less discussed publicly. Greenpeace had made sporadic attempts to place environmental concerns on the global agenda, but these attempts, although laudable, had never been very successful.

The Big Three had kept producing automobiles with fins and chrome and powered by engines with little or no regard to emissions or fuel consumption. Fossil fuel, in those days, had been considered a nondepleting asset, with supply greatly outpacing demand. And yet, Gordon had had a vision. He had foreseen that the world would change and had been ready to create a car company. The success of his proposed business was based on the dual strategy of energy conservation and environmental protection; neither issue had perceived strategic advantage at the time. Either Gordon Welsh was a great visionary or an idealistic fool.

At first, the business segment of the population had been skeptical, to say the least, of Gordon's announced strategy. Yet Gordon had the reputation of being a hard-nosed businessman with a sixth sense for a profitable opportunity, and so, though the public had not shared Gordon's optimism over his new venture, they had not been ready to dismiss it as a frivolous pipe dream either. They had looked at it with curiosity and interest.

Many had invested in the initial public offering when Gordon went to the public markets to raise capital for the start-up of Santius Automotive Inc. The media had found in Gordon a messiah-type business leader who had precisely captured, in Santius's strategy, the two most important issues that would define our world in the next fifty years: fuel efficiency and environmental care.

The media had followed Gordon everywhere, printing his every pronouncement as if it were emanating from the Holy Scriptures. And

Gordon had known how to play the media to further his interests. He knew what they wanted to hear; therefore, he had uttered thoughts that were controversial, scandalous, patriotic, or encouraging, all as circumstances required. This media frenzy had been partially—some might say, principally—responsible for an oversubscribed initial public offering. Santius Automotive Inc. had become a reality, and with the funds from the successful IPO, Gordon had been ready to roll out his vision.

When Mark first began to work with Santius, the company had been in operation for almost twenty years. Gordon had never strayed from his early strategy and the mandate he had implemented. Even when it looked as if Gordon may have misconceived future global automotive needs, Santius kept creating small automobiles that were at least twice as fuel efficient as those of its competitors and were infinitely more eco-friendly than any other car.

As the world entered the twenty-first century, and as certain world conflicts began to create global unrest, spikes in fuel prices began to surface, at first sporadically and later with more regularity. From time to time, there was wild panic in some parts of the world over the unavailability of gasoline. As the media focused on long lines, and "we are out of gas" signs appeared at many service centers, Gordon's legend as a visionary grew in stature. And so did Santius's car sales and profitability.

As the price of energy continued to fluctuate, at times with dramatic volatility, the discomfort consumers felt over the unpredictability of supply and price only increased consumers' demands for smaller and more fuel-efficient automobiles. This change in consumer pattern forced a number of automobile manufacturers to adopt Gordon's strategies, implemented twenty years earlier. It was now beginning to seem that Gordon had created a market niche that would ensure, or at lease prolong, the Santius brand's competitive advantage.

CHAPTER 3

Early one Monday morning, Mark's phone rang. "Good morning. This is Mark Gentile," Mark said.

"Mark, it's Gordon. Can you come to the offices tomorrow?" The urgency in Gordon's voice raised Mark's curiosity over the nature of the proposed meeting, but the veteran executive didn't bite. "I want to talk to you about something that can't easily be discussed on the phone," Gordon said. "Come by at ten o'clock tomorrow morning— and set aside the whole day."

Mark asked his long-time assistant, Jennifer Cole, to cancel all his appointments for the next day. The fact that there had been no unnecessary preliminary chitchat, and that Gordon's request had left no room for Mark's refusal to attend, created a sense of anticipation and excitement in Mark.

"Good to see you again, Mark. Please sit down," Gordon said as Mark entered the private conference room adjacent to Gordon's office the next day. Mark poured coffee for himself and Gordon and sat across from the CEO at the small round table.

"Mark, I'll get right to the point. There's much for us to discuss today, and for you to consider." Mark's anxiety was palpable as a light throb in his head began like the distant beating of a drum. Nevertheless, his demeanor was calm, professional, and attentive. Gordon began his narrative slowly and reflectively.

"When I conceived Santius's strategy twenty plus years ago, I knew—well, perhaps that's too strong a word—let's say that I strongly suspected that energy would eventually become the world's most pressing issue. Over one half of the world's population lives in unimaginable levels of poverty, so, sooner or later, I knew natural progress would dictate an emergence, a development, of these markets. Countries like China, India, Brazil—accounting for one-half of the world's population—were necessarily going to emerge and become industrialized. This evolution required energy, more energy than was available, more energy than was conceivable. Imagine the development of infrastructures to accommodate almost three billion persons. Cars, factories, roads, houses, commercial facilities, machinery, equipment—all needing energy from a depleting source.

"Today, and for the foreseeable future, the thirst for energy by these emerging markets, coupled with the continuing and ever-increasing need for energy by the developed nations, is wreaking havoc in our environment through increased emissions. This need for energy is dramatically increasing the price of fossil fuel beyond affordability. I felt, and still feel, that this could plunge the world into an economic depression the likes of which our world has not experienced."

Mark listened intently and marveled at the simplicity of Gordon's common sense. *Why hasn't anyone else articulated this analysis with the same matter-of-fact logic and simplicity?* Mark thought. *It is so persuasive precisely because there seems to be precious little to rebut. That's what distinguishes a visionary like Gordon from the rest of us.*

Gordon sipped his coffee and continued. "This was the underpinning for the creation of Santius. Although it's still too early to tell definitively, I believe Santius's strategy was well-conceived. And as an affirmation of that strategy, I am comforted by the fact that all the world's automobile manufacturers are now becoming more and more intent on producing fuel-efficient and environmentally friendly cars. And I am also comforted by the fact that Santius has become an extremely profitable company. We have happy shareholders, Mark. We have plenty of retained earnings and plenty of free cash with which to pay the increasingly more substantial legal bills from Curtin & Joseph," Gordon quipped with a smile on his face.

"You have certainly created an exciting and profitable company, Gord, and, in addition, a company that serves the public well and helps preserve our planet. Santius is a tremendous success story, intertwined with the risk-taking, pioneer spirit of its founder." Mark was sincere with his words. As he looked at Gordon, Mark could see a slight wetness around his eyes. The old grizzly bear had been touched by Mark's words.

Gordon's composure returned instantly. "Mark, business is different today than in the past. This is the new era of corporate governance rules under Sarbanes-Oxley; of scrutinized disclosure statements; of committees and subcommittees; of class actions through unscrupulous, money-driven attorneys. Now, I'm not saying that these regulatory requirements aren't needed, but it seems that the pendulum has swung to the other side too far, too quickly. The corporate world has become too regulated in a quagmire of undecipherable and sometimes conflicting rules that make it difficult to conduct business in an entrepreneurial way, as we used to. Now, we need lawyers and accountants at every turn. Every management recommendation to the board is now delegated to a committee of lawyers, accountants, and financial analysts. Days, weeks, or even months go by without decisions being made. Everyone is afraid of a misstep so as not to have their actions appear on the radar of government regulators or, worse still, of hungry class-action attorneys. It's common knowledge these days that even an innocuous letter from a regulatory agency announcing a simple inquiry into the affairs of a company will immediately be followed by a dramatic decline in stock price, and in turn, by class actions demanding hundreds of millions, if not billions, of dollars."

Mark felt somewhat defensive at being a member of a profession that Gordon seemed to have singled out as a major contributor to the overregulation of public companies and to the current erosion of the entrepreneurial spirit that, for many years, had signaled the rise of capitalism.

"This brings our discussion to the reason I asked you to this meeting, Mark."

Mark had been so intellectually stimulated by Gordon's analyses that he was ready to jump out of his skin. Instead, he said calmly, "Gord, there's a lot of truth to what you're saying. I'm ready to help in any way I can." Gordon's pragmatism gave him an air of efficiency. Mark noticed, however, that the discussion seemed to have depleted Gordon of his usual energy. Mark didn't know whether to attribute this to simple physical fatigue or to some unspecified physical or emotional setback. It was clear, though, that Gordon had something important to say and that he was quite determined to say it as quickly as possible.

"Mark, I've been following your legal career very closely over the last few years. I have retained you to provide Santius with your valuable legal counsel from time to time, and you have impressed me with your maturity, not simply as a lawyer, but also, and more importantly, as a businessperson. You have struck me as someone who has a vision beyond day-to-day legal issues. There is a risk-taking edge about you that's controlled and yet aggressive. I've concluded that, at this important point in time, Santius needs an infusion into its senior ranks with the type of youthful maturity that you can offer. I want to discuss a major career opportunity for you, but first, we'll have to take a break so I can make a couple of phone calls. Then we'll retire to the dining room and continue our meeting over lunch."

CHAPTER 4

After Gordon left the conference room, Mark sat motionless, stunned by the CEO's last comments. His mind started to fluctuate uncontrollably, like a bee darting from flower to flower in search of its best food target. These thoughts wandered to his law school graduation ceremony; to his first nervous days as a young prosecutor; to his initial Curtin & Joseph experience as a business litigator; to his subtle, but, nonetheless, real transition into corporate-commercial work. These steps, Mark reasoned, were all progressions, stepping stones, to an eventual—as yet unrealized—position of control, power, and influence, wherein he would employ his considerable legal skills and his acquired commercial knowledge to an end that was destined to be much more important and multidimensional than his tenure as a legal advocate.

Mark often dreaded the end of his legal retainers. He was never totally satisfied in simply giving legal or strategic advice and ending his involvement with the rendering of an invoice for his services. He wanted to be involved in the implementation of his advice and to be accountable, and hold others accountable, for the results; he wanted to be in control of the strategy and not just a contributor to it. In short, Mark wanted to be an executive who was seen as a true leader who commanded the respect of his staff, his peers, and his company's shareholders. Mark often thought of himself as a lawyer by training; at once the decision maker in respect to legal issues, and at the same time the executive responsible for financial matters and the overall strategic direction of a public company. Nothing would ultimately please Mark more than to create a powerful and profitable enterprise through both his hard work and that of his assembled team.

But Mark had, until now, believed he needed more seasoning and corporate maturity before embarking on that voyage. Was he reading too much into Gordon's flattering words? Was Gordon on the verge of realizing Mark's dream ahead of schedule? And if Gordon was, in fact, offering him a senior executive role in Santius, would Mark be prepared to jump at the opportunity? Or should he, out of an abundance of caution, take a rain check until he was certain he could step in and succeed?

As Mark visualized the life of a litigator and that of an executive, as his mind fluctuated from Curtin & Joseph to Santius and back again, Mark heard himself whispering Yogi Berra's famous line, "When you reach a fork in the road, take it."

Mark knew, at that moment, that regardless of which of Yogi's two forks he followed, his success would be assured. There was no need to fret unduly over which of the two paths to follow. When it was time for him to make a decision, Mark would follow only the recommendation of his closest adviser: his instinct.

Mark looked at his watch and realized that Gordon had been absent for less than ten minutes. His mind had traveled great distances in that short period of time.

CHAPTER 5

Over tuna sandwiches and salads, Mark and Gordon resumed their discussion.

Mark was now anxiously weighing every word uttered by Gordon, probing every intonation and dissecting his every movement, no matter how miniscule or seemingly insignificant.

"Mark, I want—Santius wants—you to join our senior executive team immediately. For the first three months, you would hold the title of senior vice president of legal and strategic affairs. You would be involved in every aspect of the operations—legal, strategic, financial, administrative, and operational—to give you a full opportunity to learn all aspects of the business. You would attend every important meeting with me, and you would participate in every internal and external event in which I am involved."

Mark's mind was racing at full speed, and he could hear his heart thumping in his chest. *This is the ultimate executive grooming*, Mark thought. It seemed as if Gordon was planning for his immediate successor with urgency. But Mark couldn't fathom why the founder of Santius, its strategic mind and power since inception, would want to relinquish the reins of power and influence so abruptly.

As Mark began to search for these answers, Gordon resumed, "Within four months, Mark, I expect Santius's board, on my strong recommendation, to appoint you as my successor. It will be your responsibility to ensure that Santius continues to be a viable, ethical, and profitable entity for many years to come."

As controlled as Mark wanted to appear, his face expressed only disbelief. "I know this is short notice, Mark, but my circumstances have dramatically accelerated the need to appoint a successor." Gordon paused to gather his thoughts. "Our board set up a search committee to review a short list of candidates. But we, as a committee, unanimously concluded that you're the person Santius needs at the helm during this next important phase of its corporate existence."

There were many questions Mark wanted to ask: What were Santius's expectations? What influence would Mark have in selecting his own senior management team? What specific priorities had Gordon and the board established for him? However, believing that these questions did not ultimately affect his decision, Mark walked around the conference table, took Gordon's hand, tightened his grip, and said genuinely, "Gord, your trust in me is overwhelming. I'm deeply honored, and I look forward to working closely with you over the next few months. I will continue to seek your advice and take advantage of your experience and wisdom. I'll never forget that Santius is your company and that your say will always have an influence on its direction, so long as I am in a position to allow it." Mark's words touched Gordon, and for the first time, Mark saw the physical frailty of Gordon Welsh. It almost seemed as if Gordon had dramatically aged right before his eyes.

"Never forget," Gordon said, "that Santius belongs not to me or to any one person. It belongs to the shareholders, the risk takers. Everything we undertake as executives must be for the benefit of Santius and its shareholders-at-large, and not for the personal benefit of a few. The company must be operated strategically, in the same way you would make decisions on behalf of your own household—not for today or tomorrow, but for its long-term benefit." Gordon paused for a moment, searching for the right words.

Mark reflected carefully on Gordon's words, and concluded that he had just explained the complex legal doctrine of "fiduciary duty" in a more succinct and eloquent manner than he had read in hundreds of judicial decisions purporting to grapple with the meaning and breadth of the term.

"And make no mistake, Mark," Gordon said. "There will be overwhelming pressures on Santius's leader to take shortcuts to satisfy personal needs by camouflaging selfish ambitions with the cloak of supposed legitimacy."

Mark picked up on the theme. "You and I, Mark, will carefully monitor these types of unethical or inappropriate motives and we won't…" At this point, perhaps more prematurely than Gordon had hoped, he concluded, "I have three months, four maximum, to hand down all my knowledge and experience to you, Mark. My doctors tell me that my number has been called by the Almighty." Gordon did not elaborate further.

Mark sat speechless.

Today marked the end of an era—and, perhaps, the beginning of a new one.

CHAPTER 6

Of the several eulogies given at Gordon Welsh's funeral, Mark's was the most moving. During the last twelve weeks of his life, Gordon had spent all his energy grooming Mark for his eventual leadership at Santius. Even in the week before his passing, Gordon had worked long days with Mark, trying to provide him with as wide a spectrum of experience and involvement as possible. At times, Mark had a hard time believing that this energetic, thoughtful, and principled human being was rapidly coming to the end of his life.

Mark often thought how impossibly difficult it must have been for Gordon to go to bed at night, knowing that there would only be several more nights before his sleep would become eternal. Every experience during the fatal countdown would be considered precious because of its finality. Eating a meal, walking in the park, petting the dog, watching a favorite TV program, visiting a friend or loved one— every activity had the reality of imminently becoming his last.

And yet, while one might have readily forgiven the onset of lethargy, Gordon instead chose to spend the last of his energy working to impart to Mark his strategic vision and to pass down invaluable pearls of wisdom so as to minimize Mark's substantial learning curve. Mark often wondered how he would have reacted in Gordon's predicament and concluded that he would not have been able to simulate Gordon's final days. Mark was more epicurean, less stoic. He would likely not have had the same corporate commitment. Mark would have wanted to spend his last days with family and friends rather than with some young lawyer, grooming him to assume control of the company he had founded.

On the other hand, he reasoned, Santius was more than a corporate entity to Gordon. Santius had become so intertwined with Gordon's very being that one was a mirror image of the other. Gordon had spent his last days doing exactly what he had wanted to do. Mark was fortunate to have been the beneficiary of Gordon's experience, knowledge, and incredible commitment.

When Mark assumed the mantle of leadership, he decided he would never contradict Gordon's principles, his integrity, or any of the lessons he had taught him.

"My friends," Mark concluded in his eulogy, "Gord was a remarkable man. He was like a father to me. Over the last few weeks of his life on this earth, he gave me advice that I will forever treasure and that I wish to share with you today." The church was overflowing with family, friends, colleagues, peers, Santius shareholders, bankers, and professionals.

"Gord operated this company in the same way he lived his life, with integrity and passion and in a manner he found fulfilling. He led his professional life to the fullest, but he also loved his family and continually sought to achieve a happy balance between his two life priorities."

Many in the audience nodded with understanding. Others wept silently.

"But perhaps Gordon's most honorable trait was his sense of fairness and his moral fiber. Whether watching a football game, leading corporate activities, or dealing generally with life's vicissitudes, Gordon always believed it was important to succeed—but only if success came with fairness and integrity. Otherwise, the price was too high."

"These are the criteria that defined Gordon Welsh's life. These are the principles that Gordon taught me so generously. These same principles will govern my own life both as an executive of the company he founded, and as a person.

"May God bless you, Gordon, my friend..."

CHAPTER 7

Mark's honeymoon with Santius's analysts lasted only a few months. The economic outbreak had darkened with a rapidity not seen since the last recession of the 1980s. Almost overnight, it seemed, the volatility index, used to gauge the public's confidence level with the economy, had risen fourfold from its historic levels. People were concerned about the security of their jobs and what tomorrow would bring.

As a result, a domino effect took hold in quick succession: people began easing up on their spending; big ticket items like automobiles and houses remained unsold and substantially grew in inventory; and job layoffs ensued, thus further reducing consumer confidence and, therefore, consumer spending.

These factors, and others, were followed by a dramatic cutback in corporate, consumer, and banking activities. The markets began to tumble as equity holders sold off their positions and retreated to the safety of Treasury bills and corporate bonds. In turn, this reduced economic activity spread from the United States and Canada to other parts of the world and soon became a global recession with reduced corporate activity. Energy inventory levels increased due to lack of consumption. Oil prices fell precipitously to levels that had not been seen in over five years. Even at twenty-five dollars a barrel, oil inventories grew, further reducing the price of the commodity. All of a sudden, Santius's strategic advantage of manufacturing small, fuel-efficient cars vanished as the cost of a fill-up dropped dramatically. Consumers were no longer concerned about fuel efficiency, it seemed, when oil prices were so low. Nor was there much concern about fuel emissions and their impact on the environment. People worried about the security of their jobs rather than the effect of global warming on the rapidly melting glaciers in Antarctica.

Santius's uninterrupted record of growth stalled, and its stock price retreated. In these turbulent times, Mark's legendary tenacity and creativity needed to shine. He decided he would welcome the current economic collapses and turn them into an opportunity.

Mark had, for some time, considered a new strategic direction for Santius, and had confidentially discussed it with his most trusted senior managers. It was now time to begin the process that would determine its feasibility and, ultimately, its implementation.

Nevertheless, as bleak as things seemed, Santius fared better than its larger competitors. Its substantially lower price point for its cars, coupled with some aggressive marketing and customer incentives, allowed Santius to at least break even in profitability. Although far from ideal, Gordon's long-standing strategy was once again proving to be a corporate lifesaver.

CHAPTER 8

With the assistance of Merkson LLC, a nationally renowned consulting company, Mark initiated a thorough and objective analytical survey of Santius's current strategy, its employees, and its management. The first objective of the survey was to determine the company's future viability by reviewing its current corporate objectives. Then, the survey would determine whether the current direction should continue untouched, whether it needed minor tweaking, or, as Mark strongly believed, whether it was time for Santius to dig into its historic entrepreneurial roots and devise a new and creative path.

In order to preserve the integrity of the process, Mark's views would be gathered by Merkson in the same way other opinions from management were collected: through thorough, all-encompassing market due diligence and a personal interview process. Mark did not wish to unduly influence the analysis. His views would count and certainly be more influential than those of others, but they would be offered and gathered fully within the parameters of the process that applied to every other contributor. Gordon would not have wanted the process to be carried out any other way.

In Mark's interview with Merkson, his views were clear, decisive, and persuasive. "Santius needs to engage in a new direction in order to preserve the vision of its founder. We need to use our current surplus cash flow to move into the era of alternative energy," he said thoughtfully. "We need to cut back, or even eliminate, our stock dividends for the next two or three years. Perhaps we should also increase our corporate debt, all with a view toward producing a new type of automobile—one that's fueled by biofuels, those environmentally friendly energy sources that are produced by agriculture and wood waste." Mark went on to advise the consultants that such technology already existed and that sample pilot batches, and even some commercial plants, were now being quietly produced to confirm the products' efficiencies.

"Continuing to produce cars run by fossil fuel will be a grave error. As oil prices inevitably increase over time, all major car manufacturers will engage in Santius's strategy of producing smaller and more efficient gasoline-driven engines. Santius will lose its edge and will be squeezed out by its more corpulent competitors. We must stay ahead of the competition and immediately transition to biofuel-driven engines. In addition to ensuring Santius's viability, we'd also be taking an important step to preserve our environment and to make the world more energy self-sufficient. The gamble is substantial. The rewards are immense." At the conclusion of his interview, he provided the consultants with a summary of the key points he had discussed and his projected details and time lines for the proposed strategy conversion.

Mark had personally done substantial research on the advantages of biofuels produced from biomass as an alternative transportation fuel. He had concluded that liquid biofuels had many advantages over other forms of energy sources. They were efficient, cost-effective, and used nondepleting wastes. In other words, these types of biofuels interfered with neither the food chain nor other existing fuels. They used waste: wood chips, straw, grasses, food waste, diseased trees, and bushes. In short, their ingredients were the refuse that's all around us. They were a nondepleting resource that did not harm, or detract from, the environment.

These types of biofuels seemed to be, according to Mark, the perfect energy sources that could be produced efficiently and could replace, or drastically diminish, the consumption of gasoline. As such, these fuels would become the market niche that would indefinitely ensure Santius's future financial and corporate success.

After three weeks of intensive work, the consultants submitted a report to Mark and Santius's board, essentially affirming Mark's proposed new direction. The report, nevertheless, emphasized that while the conversion from fossil fuel-driven energies to alternative energies would, in the long-term, preserve Santius's viability and profitability, in the short-term, there would be a substantial earnings reduction, massive CAPEX—capital expenditures—investment, and, concomitantly, much higher corporate debt. The clean, debt-free balance sheet, of which Santius had been proud for so long, would, for a few years at least, be a thing of the past. Necessarily, the consultants argued, the share price would fall substantially beginning almost immediately following the announcement. Also, in order to preserve its cash for investment in these new technologies, Santius's generous dividends would need to be suspended indefinitely.

Upon receiving Merkson's draft report, Burton Cavendish, chairman of the board, called an urgent board meeting for a preliminary discussion of the issue.

"Gentlemen," he began, "while there will be a full opportunity to consider the issues canvased in the report later, I wanted to raise two important issues right now. First, it is imperative that the contents of this report be kept strictly confidential until the company, through our disclosure committee, determines if and when to go public. If there were to be any premature leaks of the report's contents, we can all speculate about the effect they would have on our stock price.

"Second, and I am directing this request to Mark, the board needs to consider the report's conclusion and recommendations together with a full and detailed five-year financial pro forma, setting out an analysis of expenses for the transition, revenues during the period, and resulting corporate earnings, year-over-year, for each of the next five years. Though the consultants have indicated a 20 percent reduction in revenues over the first three years, a resurgence to current levels of revenues and profits in year four, and a 40 percent revenue increase by the end of year five, the board will want these financial issues carefully considered and reconsidered by senior management, and then affirmed by our auditors."

Cavendish's requests were reasonable and prudent, and Mark welcomed the opportunity to work with his financial team to go through every detail to ensure that a full financial analysis would be submitted to the board.

But Cavendish wasn't finished. "I'm sure we all understand that if this recommendation is followed, it would require an important internal marketing spin to maintain the company's morale throughout the admitted collapse of the stock price, and to preserve, as much as possible, our loyal shareholder base. A lowering of morale would undoubtedly result in the loss of key employees and difficulty in hiring future talent. A stock collapse would endanger everything, including the company's current financial structures, existing bank loans, and overall credibility with its investors, bankers, and shareholders."

Cavendish's warning, although overly negative, had a degree of legitimacy. No one could question that the new strategy entailed a difficult three or four years for the company, and it was impossible to predict all the potentially negative repercussions that could result from this redirection.

Cavendish was right in pointing out these negatives. But there was an edge to the chairman's voice, an antagonistic tone, that led Mark to suspect that Cavendish would become his aggressive adversary in this process, and that soon a line in the sand would be drawn by the two combatants.

Mark thought about the lessons he had learned from his deceased mentor. Act at all times with ethics and integrity. Act in the best long-term interests of the company. Don't be influenced unduly by the stock price. Operate the company judiciously and prudently, and the stock price will look after itself. As Mark had promised Gordon, these would be the criteria that would guide his tenure as leader of Santius, and the principles that would also guide him as a person.

The time when Mark's integrity and resolve would be tested was approaching faster than he had ever imagined.

CHAPTER 9

Burton Cavendish was sixty-nine years old. He had a storied academic, professional, and business career. Five years after he'd obtained his law degree from Yale, summa cum laude, he received his MBA from the Rotman School of Management in Toronto.

Cavendish had dabbled in corporate law for three years at one of Wall Street's most prestigious law firms—but had soon realized his calling was to make decisions as a principal, rather than implementing decisions made by his clients. As a result, he had joined Merkson, the country's most prestigious consulting firm, where for three years he honed his skills as an up-and-coming entrepreneur, fluent in interpreting financial statements. After his brief training at Merkson, he had joined one of their largest clients—Canerg Inc.—an oil refinery firm whose main focus was the development of a patch of the Alberta Oil Sands. Within seven years, Burton Cavendish had become the company's CEO.

In the ensuing decade, Cavendish dutifully followed the mandate given to him by Canerg's board of directors: invest heavily in the development of the oil sands. Cavendish had independently concluded that U.S. enemies were set to flex their muscles and challenge the premier status of the hitherto unchallenged world economic and military leader. They would use oil, he figured, as their ultimate weapon, a weapon so strategically important that it could well bring down fifty years of uninterrupted U.S. progress and power and, indeed, U.S. economic, social, and military dominance.

After becoming CEO, Cavendish introduced an employee stock option plan that served to boost pride and internal talent. The plan evolved in the beginning as the company's earnings skyrocketed year after year. These earnings increases, in turn, resulted in a rapid acceleration of Canerg's stock price and every employee benefited from this seemingly continuous windfall.

To bolster the sense of ownership from the highest executive to the stock room clerk, Cavendish had proudly installed a stock performance monitor in Canerg's reception area which digitally displayed, in real time, Canerg's stock performance, minute by minute. During the more exciting events, small groups of employees gathered to observe the continuing upswings—sometimes slow and at other times accelerated. Cavendish took pride in seeing how Canerg was positively changing the lives of so many of its sons and daughters. As a result of this prolonged and uninterrupted success, Canerg attracted the brightest minds to its corporate ranks. This, in turn, served to guarantee a continuation of its amazing success. Those were the wonder years, when it seemed nothing could go wrong and every strategic venture Cavendish initiated or approved turned into huge profits for the company and its shareholders.

Cavendish's place in the corporate world as one of Canada's most successful CEOs had been assured, or so it seemed. He routinely ranked as a finalist in many of the contests for "CEO of the Year" and "Entrepreneur of the Year." And on one occasion, he had proudly taken home the prize. Speakers' invitations flowed constantly, as did guest appearances for a number of worthwhile charities. Cavendish had become a man of considerable influence. His personal net worth similarly rose to the level of the ultra wealthy—although, to be sure, it was "paper wealth." Cavendish's Canerg holdings had elevated him to the prestigious status of being in the top 250 of the wealthiest North Americans. His estimated wealth was in excess of five billion dollars, and with Canerg's continued growth, it was likely that, within three to five years, he would edge into the elite club of the one hundred wealthiest people in the world. This was a goal that seemed to preoccupy Cavendish endlessly. The more he had, the more he wanted. His ambition was all-consuming. But his corporate drive was never based on nationalistic pride; rather, it was a corporate objective colored almost solely by subjective goals, particularly money. While it appeared as if he had sought to advance the best interests of Canerg's shareholders, in fact, he had pursued the growth of his personal Canerg portfolio, evidenced by the rather substantial shareholding he had accumulated mainly through cheap executive stock options.

Cavendish was a man who hated unmanageable risk. He was known by his closest allies as a fiscally prudent businessman. While Canerg's CEO, he did mental calculations, several times a day, on the upward and downward fluctuations of his personal wealth based on the upticks and downticks in Canerg's stock price. He despaired when Canerg's stock plummeted and enthusiastically celebrated its upswings. Perhaps his ultraconservatism or, as he called it, his prudence, was ingrained from his years as a corporate attorney who had often advised his overeager clients to temper their exuberance in favor of safer and more predictable routes.

The oil sands project, however, had put the brakes on Canerg's growth. Cavendish had had misgivings in approving his company's entry into this speculative venture. On the one hand, Canerg continued to show profit and potential from its refinery business. On the other hand, it was unmistakable that the oil industry had become a political balloon, being kicked this way and that to satisfy the political interests of a few privileged countries and the personal whims and ambitions of their leaders. However, he had been persuaded to invest in the oil sands by his top advisers, who had foretold doom and gloom in the oil refinery industry. "We must diversify, we need to keep up with the times," he had been told. "After all, the Japanese, the Chinese, and even the Russians are investing heavily in the oil sands." The world was indeed changing rapidly. Events were becoming unpredictable. Oil spikes or collapses had become a weekly, even daily, concern that substantially impacted the availability of crude oil and, therefore, the supply of the finished product.

Up until that point, Canerg had been able to override market fluctuations by stockpiling crude at unprecedented rates. In fact, the increased stockpiled inventory not only permitted Canerg to honor its supply commitments to its customers, but also allowed it to charge its customers the ever-increasing price for its refined oil—all legitimately done in accordance with evolving market conditions.

But how long will this upward spiral last before the proverbial bubble bursts? Cavendish thought at the time. *Every few years, technological breakthroughs alter the world order. Will this inevitably happen with oil? Will the recent talk about protecting the environment, the accelerated development of alternative energy sources, and consumer revolts against elevated gasoline prices continue to create unpredictability in the supply and stability of oil prices? Could a severe global recession take hold as a result of the volatility, and therefore the unaffordability, of energy?*

And so, with all these thoughts, arguments, and contrarian views swirling in his head, Cavendish made the ultimate decision. Canerg joined the ranks of forward-looking nations to invest in the largest oil deposits in the world—the Alberta Oil Sands. Cavendish believed that Canerg's investment and risk-taking would be rewarded handsomely in the following years.

But some three years later, the optimism of becoming a dominant energy leader had turned into a frantic reconsideration of Canerg's involvement in the oil sands. The company had invested over two billion dollars in equipment, manpower, and engineering development, without even a hint of when a return on investment would begin. During that time, Canerg saw its market capitalization drop by one billion dollars.

Some of the best financial, mining, energy, and oil-drilling minds on the planet were on permanent retainers to provide progress reports, financial analyses, pro forma statements, and forecasted future earnings. Cavendish had used these reports at every quarterly earnings conference call to assuage tough questions from analysts and respond to the increasing wrath of Canerg's shareholders who had grown tired of the downward spiraling of their return on investment.

For three long years, Cavendish waited for a ray of hope from the analyses. How long would this depression last? By worrying about his own eroding Canerg portfolio, Cavendish was expressing dissatisfaction on behalf of the hundreds of frustrated Canerg shareholders. There was no conflict, no breach of fiduciary duty to his employer, no selfishness on his part, he had concluded. His interests in wanting to see a performing stock were identical to those of his co-shareholders. Morale within Canerg, from the top down, was at an all-time low. Cavendish felt it was his corporate and ethical duty to do everything possible to reverse the situation.

Cavendish wished he had been more prudent, instead of being swayed by the theoreticians who treated important corporate analyses like a PhD thesis. Had he followed his gut, instead of the trends, Canerg would have continued to thrive financially, and its shareholders would have continued to enjoy profits from their shareholdings. And, of course, coincidentally, Cavendish's personal net worth would not have taken such a dramatic beating.

But although Cavendish had desperately wanted to abandon what he firmly believed had been a reckless and risky misadventure, the reality was that because of all the capital commitments that had been made by Canerg, there was no way out for at least two years. The only hope was a miraculous development breakthrough. But Cavendish did not believe in miracles—at least when they involved corporate strategies. Miracles would not be available to salvage the financial quagmire in which Canerg had sunk. What needed to be done was to exit the project as quickly as possible and at the least financial expense.

Cavendish had decided that unless he immediately terminated the oil sands project, the very financial viability of Canerg was at risk. No company, not even a powerhouse like Canerg, could continue to spend in excess of one billion dollars annually without any foreseeable return on its investment. The reality, his financial advisers had told him, was that Canerg had gone from being cash rich to now needing to access its substantial lines of credit to finance the project.

Going to the equity markets was out of the question. Canerg's shareholders would never permit financing that would inevitably dilute every shareholder's equity position. Cavendish had been fortunate to get their approval for the last equity infusion of capital. And so, Cavendish stopped all future commitments beyond the current contracted obligations, signaling to the outside world the imminent end of Canerg's involvement in the oil sands. Nevertheless, Canerg was contractually compelled to fund its commitments for the next two years, to the tune of one billion dollars per year. Aggressiveness and ambition came at a high price.

Cavendish swore to himself that if he could extricate Canerg from this misguided venture, he would never again allow himself to be swayed away from staying on a course that had been tried and true. Desperately, Cavendish tried to find moneyed partners for the project, but there were no takers. It was generally known in the financial and energy circles that Canerg was in a cash crunch and the vultures were circling, ready to pounce and share the rotten carcass that would be Canerg.

In the meantime, the price of crude oil continued to be volatile. As a result, Canerg's strategy of acquiring huge amounts of inventory to meet the demands of its customers became more difficult to attain; Canerg simply no longer had the cash to buy surplus inventory. Additionally, suppliers of crude tightened their credit to Canerg and began to insist on cash on delivery. Banks refused to extend further lines of credit and began to scrutinize Canerg's contractual covenants to find loopholes that would allow them to demand immediate repayment of their loans.

There seemed to be no way out. Canerg's acquisition of crude virtually stopped. Its temporary survival demanded that it unlock its reserved inventory. Production in its refineries was cut back dramatically. Customers who, until quite recently, had pledged their loyalty to Canerg because of its stability and dependability, now sought and found other financially stable suppliers. All these corporate maladies were, of course, soon reflected in the company's depreciating stock price which was at a ten-year low.

The erosion in Canerg's stock price had several immediate negative impacts. First, Canerg canceled its stock dividends. As a result, many loyal shareholders reinvested in other dividend-paying stocks, which, in turn, further depreciated the Canerg stock price. Second, all potential financing came to an abrupt end; Canerg could no longer find suitable revenue-generating acquisitions to replace diminishing refinery revenues and to replenish the coffers being emptied by the oil sands financial commitments. The short sellers of Canerg's stock were having a field day.

For Cavendish personally, the low stock price was reaching the panic point; a substantial number of his stock options were coming "underwater." All those years of meticulous planning and hard work to build his personal fortune were now destined to wipe hundreds of millions of dollars from his net worth. *At this rate,* Cavendish sardonically mused, *I'll be reduced to being a "run-of-the-mill" millionaire, rather than earning my place in the global multibillionaire club.*

October twenty-first was a glorious autumn morning, but, as it turned out, a day that Burton Cavendish would never forget. As he drove to his office early in the morning to face another depressing day of answering the same questions posed by analysts, of trying to calm the fears of Canerg's bankers, and of dealing with the continuing upward spiraling of the oil sands expenses and the downward spiraling of generated revenues, he heard on the radio a news report that almost took his breath away.

"There has been a terrorist attack on the oil fields in Kuwait and Saudi Arabia that has destroyed about 50 percent of those producing oil wells," the reporter announced. The report speculated that the North American stock markets would not open as scheduled until further news filtered in. "The markets in Europe and Asia have ceased all trading."

Fear and panic that this incident would drive the oil prices out of control gripped the world. This was aggravated further by the certainty that speculators would seize this windfall opportunity to wreak havoc through speculation. Speculation was frenzied and wild, but the reality was that nobody knew what these developments would entail. Most experts were unanimous that the world was so dependent on oil that losing the Saudi Arabian and Kuwaiti supplies would create unaffordably high oil prices that would grind the world economies to a halt, and thereby bring on a catastrophic depression, the likes of which had never been seen.

The impact of the news was ruthless, surgical, and almost instantaneous. When markets reopened, chaos and panic reigned. The price of oil quickly escalated to over two hundred dollars a barrel and continued to climb; virtually no one could afford to remain in business. No one was buying and therefore no one was selling. The stock markets lost 75 percent of their value and billions of dollars were wiped away.

No one was spared. People were in disbelief. Those who could personally draw comparisons said, without hesitation, that even the Great Depression could not match the mood and economic devastation that was permeating the world.

The effects on Canerg were equally swift and overwhelming. Within a month, it had used up its existing credit lines and had totally run out of cash. Cavendish cut expenses dramatically in order to survive, but it became obvious that these acts were last gasp efforts. It was like wearing a life jacket in the eye of a hurricane. Within four weeks, Canerg no longer was. It was forced into bankruptcy, principally by Canerg's oil sands creditors.

What an ironic twist, thought Cavendish. *The soaring eagle that was Canerg has now been grounded and destroyed by the overly ambitious oil sands launching pad.*

And so it happened that the great Burton Cavendish lost his job, his wealth, his prestige, his social status, and his personal dignity. All gone in a flash.

Cavendish swore that he would reestablish himself and that he would never allow that type of devastation to happen to him again. *Going forward, I will always trust my initial instincts*, Cavendish promised himself. *I will always be a slave to financial prudence and stay the course of predictability.*

CHAPTER 10

Aboard meeting to discuss the Merkson report was scheduled for a week after Cavendish's emergency meeting. Mark was confident that a full and equitable top-down process had been implemented by the best management consulting firm money could buy. The process had involved internal interviews first with senior executives, then with middle management operational and marketing executives, and lastly with managers. Merkson employed financial models using conservative, aggressive, and normal marketing and sales assumptions, all plugged into the research and development pipeline forecasts for new products.

Even the administrative staff had been asked for their input. All the angles had been covered. All opinions had been sought—especially the contrarian views—to ensure that all the arguments, pro and con, had been considered. All this information had been collected, organized, and finally sifted into a clear Merkson recommendation that, if accepted by the board of directors, would have the effect of dramatically transforming the future mandate, operations, and performance of Santius. In brief, Merkson's recommendation would forever change

Santius's direction from one of certainty and future predictability, to one of uncertain, but high, potential.

Mark believed strongly in the integrity of the process Merkson had undertaken, and categorically accepted its recommendations. All that was left was convening a board of directors' meeting and make a full presentation—a "dog-and-pony show" with all the bells and whistles. Mark had been through many such presentations and knew exactly how to maximize their effect. He would ensure that a detailed summary of the key findings was outlined in a booklet. No detail would be overlooked or omitted from the presentation. The board of directors' presentation would be full and transparent. Mark did not want to leave any room for doubt among the board of directors. The strategic switch needed to be accepted on its merits as inevitable and as the only viable course for the survival of a niche player like Santius.

A few days before the scheduled presentation, Mark asked Jennifer to bring him the personal biographies of each Santius director. He wanted to make certain that he knew his audience—their personal profiles; their educational backgrounds; and, therefore, their individual ability to understand and digest engineering, mechanical, and financial complexities. He had learned years ago as a young legal advocate that winning meant not only making a compelling presentation, but also knowing your audience and adapting your advocacy to suit their needs.

Mark flipped through each file. He wanted to know the personal net worth of each director and the number of Santius shares and stock options they each held, for this would forewarn him of each director's risk appetite. Mark was determined to know these important details in order to form a picture of the self-interests of each director and, therefore, their receptiveness to his admittedly risky proposal.

Santius's board of directors was composed of seven directors, including Mark. Tony Ruprech, his hand-picked chief operating officer, was Mark's ally on the board. Tony had been instrumental in carrying out the strategic review and proposal. Obviously, Tony's vote was secure. The other five directors, on the other hand, were all independent, at arm's length, and totally uninfluenced by management.

At this critical juncture, Mark began to second-guess the advisability of having an overwhelmingly independent board. The new area of Sarbanes-Oxley's corporate governance, as Gordon had forewarned, had seemingly sacrificed corporate efficiency in favor of process.

Mark rose from his chair and walked over to the panoramic windows in the corner of his office. Though Mark stared at the setting below, he didn't really focus on it. *Gordon was right*, he thought, *Santius has spent millions of dollars in establishing new corporate governance manuals that seem more intent on satisfying the ambitions of aggressive regulators than actually providing any sense of security either for management or for shareholders.*

Still, the attorney in Mark knew that the corporate world had been rocked by scandals of late. Practically overnight, the effects of Enron had created a new and lucrative industry made up largely of attorneys who, until this windfall, had unfulfilled personal ambitions; accounting firms which, in competition with law firms, had established entire departments of corporate governance "experts" whose only expertise was to have read the statute; and newly created governance consultants, most of whom had never actually held either management or director positions, but who, nevertheless, made a living out of lecturing about the evils of allowing senior executives to manage public companies unchecked and without control—to the detriment of supposedly unsuspecting and victimized shareholders.

Mark had at first refused to embrace these statute-imposed ideals, which, he had concluded, amounted to an expensive folly. However, a reluctant change of heart had occurred when, one year, Santius's auditors had refused to sign Santius's financial statements because the company had supposedly failed to put in place financial, legal, and disclosure controls. From that point on, Santius had become a model of corporate governance, whether or not corporately necessary. It proceeded to retain the very "experts" whom Mark had loathed, and at substantial expense.

Mark's thoughts were interrupted by the arrival of his colleague and friend Tony Ruprech. Mark quickly informed Tony of his research on the independent board members. "Cavendish will be an obstacle, Tony. He is a self-interested, ambitious man."

Mark had always been proud of his thorough and diligent research abilities, a trait learned in law school and perfected as a young, practicing attorney. "Cavendish lost his company, his net worth, and his social influence because he directed his company into an excessive investment in the Alberta Oil Sands some years back. He has already been burned once by changing strategic direction..." Mark's voice trailed off in deep reflection.

"Cavendish has made no secret of his ambition to recoup some of his past personal losses through Santius. He has accumulated a substantial share position and has a very large number of very profitable stock options. Given his past failures, it would not surprise me one bit if he opted not to stray too far from Santius's current, profitable strategy."

"Mark, he's sixty-nine years old, with over 50 percent of his options exercisable in the next two years," Tony said. "His decisions will most likely be supportive of a plan that'll stay the course and thereby maximize Santius's short-term stock price. He'll want to cash out soon. He won't want any risk."

"While this is undoubtedly true," Mark conceded, "I want to believe that every board member will ultimately fulfill his fiduciary obligations to the company and will vote in favor of a strategy that serves the best interests of all shareholders." Mark knew that this last comment was a standard textbook response. He did not at all believe his own statement.

CHAPTER 11

All the preparations for the scheduled board meeting had been completed. Materials had been sent out to the directors a full week in advance, in order for them to privately review the analysis and conclusions on which they were required to vote.

The day of the meeting arrived. Mark had left nothing to chance, and as he surveyed the meeting room, he saw the team he had put in place for the presentation. Three principals and three associates from Merkson, who had accumulated the data and performed the analyses, were prepared to speak to the transparency and thoroughness of the process and to answer any questions on the conclusions reached. Kevin Houston, Santius's chief financial officer, was present to provide a financial forecast of the intended plan, as well as the dire long-term consequences if Santius's current strategy continued without interruption.

Mark stood at the front of the room. After welcoming the board, Mark, at his persuasive best, described the competitive environment affecting the auto industry, and the underlying rationale for why Santius's strategy needed to change immediately.

"There is simply no way out for us. There is no alternative but to engage in an immediate transformation of the entire business." Mark's tone was somber.

Mark had the full attention of the board.

"It will soon no longer be sufficient to produce energy-efficient cars as in the past. Our market share will be severely tested and will soon be taken over by our more powerful competitors. Santius's very existence is at risk." Mark stopped momentarily to allow his comment to be absorbed. Each of the independent board members looked at one another incredulously and shifted in their seats. Mark could see the fear in their eyes. These were all successful executives, current and former, and none of them wanted to be part of an entity set on a downward spiral.

"We need to transition out of fossil fuel-driven cars entirely, and move into alternative energy. We must partner with alternative energy developers who are in the final stages of commercializing cellulosic ethanol and biobutanol to accommodate the expected surge in flex-fuel vehicles—FFVs—and other types of engines using these alternative biofuels. We have to make sure we carve out a long-term strategic advantage over our less flexible competitors."

Mark had been carefully monitoring the trends. He had concluded that by the year 2012, at least four prominent entities in the United States, and one in Canada, would construct full-scale commercial plants for the substantial production of these "next generation" biofuels.

Mark was certain that the world was ready for this dramatic change. New engines to accommodate higher ethanol blends—up to 85 percent—would need to be produced for FFVs. Mark wanted Santius to be in the pole position of manufacturing FFVs, while at the same time investing in the production of biobutanol, which required no engine alteration.

Mark wanted Santius to be known as the maker of the "green" automobile. He wanted the company to preserve its historical entrepreneurial character and embrace unstoppable and inevitable change. He had wanted this ever since the invention of technology platforms capable of converting waste into liquid fuel.

Mark had become convinced that the time for Santius to change its direction was now. He wanted Santius to again be known as the company that cared about the environment. Mark saw these changes to the company as advantages, with no long-term negative impact to the shareholders. Indeed, with a little patience, shareholders would be handsomely rewarded for their support.

The issue was so essential, the timing so proximate, the conclusions being recommended so dramatic, that Mark did not need to dramatize the situation or exaggerate it in order to drive his points home.

"But there will be short-term sacrifices, let there be no doubt about that," he continued. "Kevin Houston, our chief financial officer, and our colleagues from Merkson will shortly provide all the financial statistics indicating that over the next couple of years, every aspect of our business will be negatively impacted. But this is necessary pain because unless we undertake the recommended strategy immediately, our company will not survive."

Mark noticed that Cavendish's discomfort was now visible as he preoccupied himself with making notes on the stock price comparative charts that had been distributed.

"Thank you for your attention," Mark said. "I'd now like to introduce Kevin Houston, who has prepared a full financial presentation for you."

It was obvious from the body language of the board directors that they had all read and studied the report, and that the oral presentations were welcomed but hardly necessary for them to grasp the gravamen of the issues.

After an intensive two hours of presentations by Mark, Kevin Houston, and various Merkson principals, Cavendish straightened himself, stood up, and addressed his colleagues.

"What would our founder, Gordon Welsh, say if he were here today?" he began. "Gord spent his energy—no pun intended—and staked his reputation on the principle that every investor in his company must be fairly rewarded." Cavendish used the old trick of starting with an incontrovertible platitude and thereafter proceeded to stake out his position. "Of course, all companies need to change—to evolve to meet the exigencies of the times. But evolution, by definition, is not instantaneous; otherwise, it is not evolution but revolution. Evolution, by definition, is slow, methodical, and carefully meditated. Most importantly, evolution should be undertaken to ameliorate, rather than degenerate, the status quo."

Cavendish now had the full attention of the meeting. His eyes locked with Mark's and he continued. "Even if the new strategic direction being recommended by our management team were accepted by this board, Gord would have never endorsed it if it meant dramatically harming the progress and profitability that Santius has achieved through so many years of hard work. It would be irresponsible to do so. Gord would have instead opted for a gradual transition over a number of years, so as to allow the strategic evolution to occur seamlessly and to protect our corporate profit and the financial return our shareholders have come to expect."

As Cavendish took his seat and wiped the beads of perspiration from his forehead, Mark saw that Cavendish's speech had brought a sense of comfort and relief to the faces around the conference table.

Cavendish immediately adjourned the meeting without providing any further opportunity for rebuttal or debate. He asked the board members to stay behind and caucus to further consider the management's recommendations.

"The meeting of the full board will resume tomorrow morning promptly at 10:00 a.m.," Cavendish said.

"Well, we certainly know where our chairman stands on the issue," Mark whispered to Tony on their way out of the room. "You read this perfectly. We will be facing a major obstacle and, frankly, with this particular board of directors, I am not sure we can overcome it."

CHAPTER 12

That evening, as Mark relaxed after dinner, he visualized the events of the day. *Could we have done anything differently?* he wondered to himself. He concluded that every reasonable step had been taken to ensure a proper, fair, and transparent process. The rebuttal by Cavendish had been expected. Mark's only uneasiness was that Cavendish's presentation had been principally, perhaps exclusively, influenced by his personal self-interests.

Marina, Mark's childhood sweetheart and wife of thirty years, appeared out of nowhere with a bowl of freshly popped popcorn. She sat down beside him on the couch to watch the classic *Twelve Angry Men*, the story of a jury deliberation over the guilt or innocence of a young man accused of murder.

"How appropriate," Mark said to his wife. "Santius's own jury is also deliberating a life-or-death issue right now, and we'll know the verdict tomorrow morning."

CHAPTER 13

As expected, Mark had a sleepless night. He sensed that the previous day's drama would have decisive corporate repercussions and that his life was about to change dramatically. He had a premonition that his personal "evolution," as Cavendish would have preferred to call it, would begin to unfold that morning.

At precisely 6:00 a.m., Mark began to put his body through its routine abuses in his home gym. As he increased both speed and elevation on his treadmill, Mark's mind wandered ahead four hours and he visualized the board's rejection of his recommendation. Important questions would stem from such a rejection. *Will the board opt to continue Santius's current strategy and operations, or will they introduce a slow transition into the proposed change? How will these decisions be communicated to the public, including its shareholders? How will Santius's stock price react to the news when it is disclosed, whatever that news might be?* These thoughts simultaneously converged in Mark's head. However, they were all subsidiary to the one question that overwhelmed Mark: How would he react to the rejection of the management's proposed strategy—a strategy so strongly recommended by him that he had left little room for any other solution?

While the issues were clear, Mark's mind was simply too over-saturated to determine appropriate answers. There would be plenty of time to sort out these strategic and personal dilemmas.

As a young litigator, Mark had often waited, anxiously with his client, for the jury to bring out its verdict. Through experience and observation, he had learned that if the jury members looked at him or his client as they filed out of the jury room to take their seats in the jury box, a verdict in their favor would likely follow. The outward expression of emotions rarely betrayed conclusions reached by the mind.

At precisely 10:00 a.m., Mark entered the boardroom and saw that everyone else had arrived. Mark proceeded to his seat next to Cavendish, extended his hand, and greeted the chairman. "Good morning, Burton. Looks like we'll have a full house," Mark joked.

Cavendish shook Mark's hand. "There are a lot of shareholders who want our continuing assurance that their nest egg is protected and rests in good hands." He surveyed the boardroom. "Our shareholders are largely friends of our company, individuals who have entrusted their hard-earned money to Santius. It's our job as a board to make sure they're not disappointed."

While Mark clearly sensed that Cavendish had suddenly drawn the battle lines, he nevertheless instinctively knew that this was not the time to create an appearance of internal conflict between board and management.

"Patience and loyalty are two traits that are usually rewarded, Burton," said Mark. And with that comment, he moved toward his seat. While the interaction seemed to be amiable on the surface, Mark knew that the next few hours would define his corporate future.

As Cavendish took out his notes, the room fell silent. *The calm before the storm*, thought Mark. He had realized that during their entire exchange, not once had Cavendish locked eyes with him. Mark's past experience with juries forewarned him of what was about to transpire.

Cavendish called the meeting to order and immediately focused on the business at hand.

"Good morning, everyone. The independent board met at length yesterday to further consider management's report and the presentations made. First, we want to congratulate Mark and his team for the effort they have made to conduct the necessary due diligence and complete the report. It was a job extremely well done and this board is grateful and appreciative of this undertaking." Soft applause and nods of approval ensued.

"In summary, the independent board has concluded that there is merit to the recommendations made in the report. However, we have also concluded that the switch in strategy should occur seamlessly and in a tempered manner over a protracted period of time. Oil prices will continue to fluctuate—at times wildly—indefinitely. We do not see the need to endanger the financial stability of Santius, nor see any purpose in needlessly eroding the market capitalization of the company, with the immediate and total implementation of Mark's new strategy." Cavendish now personalized the proposed strategy to Mark, without any reference to the laborious and faultless process that had been undertaken by Cavendish's previous employer, Merkson.

The chairman continued with his prepared script. "Santius has always been a nimble company and will always be on the leading edge of technology and ahead of its more cumbersome competitors.

"This board is the protector of Santius's shareholders. We have been entrusted by them to safeguard their investment. We should not—indeed, we cannot—approve a course of conduct knowing that it would result in a dramatic collapse of the company's stock price. Nevertheless, we do agree that over the longer term, we must evolve into a new direction, as Mark has suggested."

Purely from the standpoint of advocacy, Mark had great admiration for Cavendish and the way he expressed a total rejection of the new strategy, while at the same time, created the impression that the board was supportive. It was a masterful performance that, unfortunately, did not consider that time was of the essence and that Santius had to either change immediately or quickly be squeezed out.

"The board wishes to express its unanimous support for Mark and his management team, and wants Mark to guide Santius, within the strategic parameters upon which we will jointly agree, through the challenging but exciting times ahead."

Alea iacta est—the die had been cast—the Rubicon had been crossed. There would be no turning back by Cavendish. Nevertheless, Mark wondered if he could continue to lead the company, and still be true to his principles of integrity and ethics.

Cavendish turned slightly toward Mark and said, "Mark, since an internal process has been earlier disclosed to our analysts and the public, we request that you immediately convene a meeting of our shareholders, fully open to the company's analysts and the media, wherein you disclose the full parameters of our internal process on this issue. You will explain that in order to remain fully competitive, Santius will be undertaking an extensive study to determine its future strategic direction. You should also provide comfort to our shareholders by explaining that management and the board are continuing to review the direction of the industry, and that positive announcements will be made in due course, but that you see no immediate change to our revenue and earnings per share forecasts, all as previously given."

Mark sat in the boardroom alone for a long time after the conclusion of the meeting. He was not surprised by what had just transpired, but he was still shocked by the finality of the verdict, a verdict that could appeal to the shareholders, but at a price that might not be justified.

Later that day, Mark sat pensively in his office with his door closed. He had given a stern instruction to Jennifer to hold all calls until further notice. A knot formed in his stomach as he began to analyze his reaction and plan his future conduct.

Mark's dilemma was seemingly insoluble. On the one hand, he could not bring himself to agree that the board's decision was taken in the shareholders' best interests, nor that any delay in the implementation of the new strategy could even remotely be considered a positive development, as Cavendish had stated. On the other hand, as chief executive officer of Santius, it was his job to convey the board's decision to the public in such a way as not to harm the company. It was his fiduciary responsibility to follow the edict of the board of directors. If Mark felt unable or was unwilling to do so, his alternative was either to resign immediately or to force a confrontation between the board and management. Of these two choices, there was no doubt in Mark's mind which route he would have to follow if it came down to it.

The conference with Santius's shareholders, analysts, and the media was scheduled ten days hence. Mark sensed that this would be his most important presentation, even more important than his first jury address years earlier.

CHAPTER 14

With Merkson's principal partner on one side and Santius's chairman of the board on the other, Mark was ready for the big announcement. Support staff—financial, manufacturing, and sales—were all sitting in the front row for Mark to direct specific questions.

That morning, Mark's mind had wandered to his early youth in Acerenza, where his character was first formed.

◆

"We go to America," a young Samuele Gentile said to his wife, Maria. "We make life better for our son Marco. This is no place for him to become rich and famous. Yes, we go to America." And while Maria had heard these words many times from her husband, and had long ago concluded that these were his pipe dreams, Samuele indeed set in motion his and his family's itinerary to the New World—America. For Samuele Gentile, "America" was either Canada or the United States, indistinguishably, but mainly Canada, a gentle country bordering the

United States where the winters were colder and the entry sponsorship requirements somewhat more lenient.

◆

Although he had only been five years of age at the time, the trip through the Apennine Mountains to the Port of Naples was now lucid in Mark's mind. He vividly recalled the *arrivederci* and *buona fortuna*, "good luck," from relatives who had congregated at the port to say their final good-byes. He remembered waving to his cousins, his aunts, and his uncles as the *Queen Federica* set sail toward Genoa, through the Strait of Gibraltar, and ultimately engaged in the long transatlantic voyage toward New York, and, ultimately, to Halifax, Canada. Mark recalled the early years in this new land. The hardships his parents went through, working at menial jobs at first, but always ready to do what it took so that their son could have a better life.

With only a few minutes to go before the start of the shareholders' meeting, Mark's mind continued to visualize his life—his high school successes, culminating in a full scholarship to Canada's most prestigious university; his early admission into law school; his pursuance of a postgraduate law degree; his marriage to Marina and the birth of their lovely Dior; his early years as a young advocate; and his rise to the top of the law profession by the time he was in his mid-thirties. *Funny thing*, Mark thought. *After decades of court advocacy, and innumerable speeches before friendly and hostile crowds, I'm able to put my mind on automatic.* And yet, he now felt an anxiety he had not experienced since his first day in court, when, as a young prosecutor, he won his first case against a notorious drug trafficker. He had felt butterflies in his gut at that time, moments before the verdict was read by the judge. Now, in a different environment, Mark felt the same tingling sensations.

Santius's large auditorium was filled to capacity. Mark looked around the room and observed that the crowd was the usual mix of "professional shareholders"—mostly older men and widows who attended this and other similar meetings. For the gentlemen, shareholders' meetings had become their new "careers," a replacement for the important appointments, bankers' meetings, and operational sessions they had suffered through during their glory days. Attending these conferences allowed them to mingle with persons they considered to be their peers and still feel part of the executive rat race from which they had so desperately wanted to escape, and which they now so sorely missed. These sessions allowed them to wear their business apparel again and feel like they were still in play.

The widows, on the other hand, with their proofs of stock ownership devolved by their late spouses tightly rolled in their Prada purses, were there because their financial advisers had recommended that they see for themselves how corporate decision making happened. This allowed the financial vultures to hide behind their clients' attendance—and the imputed knowledge they would thereby gain—in case there was a downturn in the stock price. After all, their legal defense would be that their clients had themselves participated in the meetings and had themselves permitted, or at least condoned, the negative stock performance.

There was, of course, another reason for the widows' attendance. They could feel again a sense of dignity. They had, after all, been at innumerable similar functions with their late husbands. Attending these events allowed them to relive a part of their past life in the memory of their departed loved ones. Of course, an added bonus for them was the opportunity to scan the room critically to see if, perchance, there might be a willing male target or two with whom to compare their respective portfolio performances.

Mark noticed that the media, as expected, was also there in full force. Sitting in the front rows were business newspaper and magazine reporters, some of whom had interviewed him following corporate events or the issuance of important press releases. Most of them had become friendly with Mark, mainly because they could always count on him to provide an articulate summary of points that could be easily incorporated into their reports. They liked Mark because he always spoke transparently and without double-talk.

On each side aisle of the auditorium was the television media, in pairs. A jeans- and T-shirt-clad cameraperson always stood alongside a somewhat more presentable host—presentable at least from the waist up, which was the only part that mattered for television.

Tough crowd, thought Mark. An eclectic mix of interested and anxious investors, critical media representatives, and a board of directors with whom Mark didn't see eye-to-eye, filled the auditorium seats. "Let the curtain rise," Mark said to himself.

CHAPTER 15

As the head table began to file in, the loud murmuring in the vast auditorium subsided. Cavendish took the podium, thanked everyone for attending, and made the usual introductions.

"Santius has always been considered a leader in the automobile manufacturing industry. We've accomplished this by incorporating the entrepreneurial spirits of our founder, Gordon Welsh, and his successor, Mark Gentile.

"Mark has undertaken a substantial analysis of the entire industry and our company's past, current, and future roles within it. There has been much media speculation about the future of our industry and, indeed, the future of oil production as a principal 'driver'—if you'll excuse the pun—of our industry's viability. We at Santius have decided to hold this extraordinary session to bring you up-to-date with Mark's strategy going forward. Santius has always prided itself on its transparent communication to you, its owners," Cavendish said.

How clever and maliciously misleading of Cavendish to now suggest that Santius's ongoing undertaking was "my strategy," thought Mark incredulously.

"Mark will explain to you why Santius is currently better positioned than any of its competitors, and how he intends to lead Santius and achieve, in the future, similar levels of profitability as those he has achieved in the past." As the widows and retirees broke out in a loud and spontaneous applause, Mark realized just how difficult and determined an obstacle Cavendish had become. His introduction had essentially tied Mark's hands so that he would have little choice but to follow the chairman's lead in announcing that Santius would indefinitely stay the course.

But Cavendish was not quite finished with his speech. "Santius has enjoyed twenty-eight consecutive quarters of profitability, and I am deeply committed to continuing this profitability."

Every few minutes, the experienced "deliverer of good news" paused and looked at Mark benevolently and then his audience. Another prolonged round of cheers and hand clapping erupted. Some particularly gratified shareholders even gave him, and Mark, a brief standing ovation.

"I promise you that the strategies adopted by Santius will continue to reap profits in the future, as they have in the past," Cavendish said. Following this latest commitment, the elation of the shareholders could no longer be contained. They rose as one and applauded loudly and vociferously, as the television cameras scanned the audience and captured the love-in for the late-hour business news channel.

With the audience appropriately softened and amenable, Cavendish went on to describe how Santius routinely conducted self-analyses on its operations and strategies. "The role of the board of directors—and my responsibility as chairman—is to be the guardians of your rights. In that capacity, we have carefully reviewed all of the plans and strategies presented to us by senior management and have determined that a proper balancing of priorities is in the company's and, therefore, your, best interests.

"We have heard much media discussion about the upward spiraling of oil prices, about the imminent depletion of oil reserves, and of the immediate need for the automobile industry to switch totally and irrevocably to alternative energy sources and the cars that can immediately accommodate them." Deafening silence now permeated the auditorium. Mark knew, however, that Cavendish had intentionally built up his proverbial straw man to now mercilessly demolish it.

"But I have no doubt that ten years from now, these same arguments and debates will continue to be prevalent. The reason is that there is absolutely no evidence that the world is about to run out of oil. New reserves are being developed and massive new projects are being undertaken on a continuing basis. One example, of course, is right in our backyard. The Alberta Oil Sands have an oil reserve that, potentially, could make it by far the largest deposit in the world, capable of supplying oil for generations."

Of course, he's not saying a word about the complexity, cost, or timing of the oil extraction, Mark thought. *Nor is he addressing the fact that regardless of those obstacles, the world has a new environmental consciousness that will soon drive the industry to produce cars that are not only energy efficient, but also, and most importantly, environmentally friendly.*

Nor, apparently, is this the right time for Cavendish to admit that his own company, Canerg, was driven to insolvency because of his failed bet on the success of the oil sands. This is not the time for him to worry about past failures, global warming, the extraction of "dirty oil," or any such leftist sentiments. Mark was stunned by Cavendish's unethical and moral depravity.

Cavendish, in a more familial and less formalistic tone, committed that he would never allow a situation to occur which involved a quick fix, especially when there was no compelling reason to do so.

"Changes in strategy," he continued, "must occur, if at all, slowly and thoughtfully so as not to endanger the very pillars of profitability on which this company was founded and in which every shareholder has placed their hard-earned money. I will never permit any switch in strategy that punishes the company and its shareholders with a precipitous drop in revenues, and, concomitantly, an unacceptable erosion of the company's stock price."

The loud gasps of horror at Cavendish's earlier pessimistic outlook soon metamorphosed into a thunderous ovation, especially when the words "I will never permit..." were boldly emphasized on the large media screen that carried his verbatim speech.

Cavendish's brilliant presentation left little doubt that Santius had to continue on the same path that had made it successful in the past, and, importantly, that Cavendish would personally make sure that it happened.

The chairman, certain that the audience was with him, thanked everyone for their attention, called a brief recess, and invited everyone to return in a few minutes to hear directly from their CEO, Mark, the person who would see to it that Santius's run as a profitable entity would continue without interruption.

As the crowd dispersed toward the refreshment table, it was clear, from the clusters of people surrounding Cavendish with smiles of approbation, that he had totally succeeded in depicting himself as their savior-protector, and that he could, and indeed must, be trusted to wield his corporate power and influence to that end.

Cavendish had successfully played on the substantial human emotions of fear of the unknown and personal greed. Each of these emotions was, by itself, a formidable obstacle, Mark reasoned. Together, their merger would prove to be the death knell of any attempt by Mark to deviate from the path so clearly defined by the chairman.

Mark furtively left the auditorium, preferring to be alone for a few moments. Deep in thought, he walked in the outside corridor. Mark had conflicting feelings on whether to admire Cavendish's tact and brilliance as an advocate, or to despise his treachery tailored by half-baked truths, incomplete assumptions, and outright misleading conclusions.

Should I make the shareholders aware of Cavendish's personal agenda in wanting to preserve the status quo? Mark thought. *Should I explain that he desperately wants to recoup the fortune he lost through Canerg, and that, given his advanced age, he can't personally afford to wait another few years for the dramatic turnaround in profitability that would certainly follow the implementation of my strategy?*

Mark decided against this approach, principally because to do so would undoubtedly create an unbridgeable chasm between management and the board of directors.

Mark wondered if he'd been too harsh in judging Cavendish's personal motives. *Perhaps*, Mark thought, *Cavendish's role as chairman of Santius is precisely to ensure that his personal interests are not at risk, to see that those very interests are aligned perfectly with those of the majority of shareholders. After all, did he not receive howls of approval when he announced Santius's decision to retain the status quo?*

While Mark was absolutely convinced that Santius's best interests—and indeed its very viability—lay in effecting the immediate change he had proposed, nevertheless, he could certainly understand why Santius's shareholders might feel more comfortable in following the current path. After all, it was the path that had allowed small, and not so small, fortunes to be built over the last many years.

Regardless, Mark had seemingly lost this battle. What was left was simply the formality of communicating the results. It was time for Mark to declare his position on the future direction of Santius. In light of Cavendish's early pronouncements, Mark's biggest task was to see whether he could, at once, follow the direction laid out by Cavendish and be true to himself and what he stood for.

Mark decided he could not follow his prepared speech; rather, he would speak from the heart. He would rely on his natural instincts as a former litigator, as he had many times in the past. Seconds before he began to speak, Mark had no idea what his final message would be, how it would be communicated, or indeed, how it would be received.

CHAPTER 16

Ladies and gentlemen, welcome back to our presentation. Over the last several years, I've led a number of meetings like this to provide you, our shareholders, with a detailed account of your company's current operations, a review of the current and future market conditions in which we operate, and a strategic preview of our proposed future strategy." As Mark paused to look over his audience, he saw many friendly faces. The shareholders looked forward to Mark's continued leadership and the continued appreciation of their Santius shareholdings.

"You need not have any fear of further charts and symbols. Our chairman, Burton Cavendish, has certainly given you a full analysis of the processes and internal self-evaluations we have undertaken over the last many weeks. Burton has given you the conclusions that I and my senior management team recommended to the board of directors, as well as the board's support of a new strategy and its decision to defer the full consideration of our recommended strategic plan. I will not therefore make any further comment on that. You, our shareholders, through the board as your elected and authorized agent, have spoken, and your company will follow the board's decision—as it was bound to follow any contrary decision reached by it. Please permit me, though, to say something very important to you in order to put into context the internal process that I directed your company to undertake.

"Santius was born out of the very simple idea that we wished to be the most creative, nimble, and exciting automotive producer in the world. We never sought to compete with the traditional automakers—indeed, we could not hope to match the pedigree and wealth of our competitors. To the contrary, our ambition was much loftier and much more rewarding: it was to find a niche in the market that we could exploit; to create fuel-efficient vehicles when fuel efficiency was not yet *de rigueur*; to create environmentally sensitive cars at a time when, long before Al Gore and Kyoto, concerns about emissions and the damage they cause to the world were the domain of crackpots, tree huggers, leftists, Greenpeace, and the media. The fact that we successfully combined unfailing profitability with a product that was actually good for our customers and the world in which we live, served to make our shareholders both financially satisfied, and, at the same time, proud to be owners of a profitable company whose mission it was to preserve our planet."

Mark saw palpable pride in the faces of the owners. He also noticed curiosity in the faces of many in the audience and knew that he had their utmost attention. "I confess that we have created mass confusion among the business conservatives who have always equated environmental sensitivity with a leftist conspiracy to bring down capitalism as we know it. Only the media and the financial analysts who follow Santius have finally resolved Santius's seeming inexplicable contradiction, by realizing that we have created a very special company indeed—a company that has provided a record number of uninterrupted positive earnings quarters and, concurrently, has not been embarrassed at being branded as the 'automaker that cares.'

"And so, my friends, it was this need to continue to be different that drove me to undertake this internal, collective confessional to ensure that our mission would be as relevant five and ten years from now as it was over two decades ago when Santius was created. Our self-evaluation, in other words, became necessary to make sure that the drivers that had been so important to our financial well-being in the past, would continue indefinitely.

"I have always personally believed that we should never be afraid of decisions that take us into the unknown, provided that the decisions are fully thought out, deliberated, and implemented with care. I have also always believed that tough decisions, if they are to be implemented successfully, must be made quickly and clinically, without second-guessing, without procrastination, and without reservation. Otherwise, there will be inevitable confusion and, therefore, a lack of focused resolution. In my experience, it is better to avoid difficult measures altogether than to implement them haphazardly, without firmness, and without conviction."

Mark began to sense some unrest within the crowd. Nevertheless, he was determined to lay out in full detail his thoughts on this most important issue, an issue that went to the very core of Santius's existence and, indeed, to Mark's own set of values and integrity.

"The process we used was faultless. It was a thorough, bottom-up analysis that affected virtually everyone in your company. This was not a process dictated by consultants or by management. Our managers and the professionals we retained coordinated many sessions to ensure that all the ideas were heard, categorized, and funneled into a system that ultimately resulted in a clear corporate recommendation. All the disciplines were engaged individually and departmentally. We heard from the financial hardliners, the liberal members of our media relations group, our operational employees, and our marketing department. We conducted studies and customer surveys. No detail was spared from scrutiny. No stone was left unturned, as the saying goes.

"At the end of it all, management concluded—I concluded—that the time was ripe for the initiation for the next important phase of Santius's existence." The audience sat motionless and grasped Mark's every word.

"We are seeing an unprecedented merger of volatile energy costs and supply, with an insatiable appetite for fossil fuels. China and

India alone, as emerging markets, account for a population of 2.5 billion who will need traditional fossil energy in increasing volume over the next ten to fifteen years. This insatiable demand will continue to cause an upward spiral in the price of oil and of natural gas. This, in turn, will create an unparalleled need for increased oil production and refining processes. Since these commodities are nonrenewable, their depletion will be accelerated. On the contrary, if OPEC, Russia, and Canada decided not to increase production to meet the demand, energy prices could rise to unfathomable levels that could result in a global recession, even a global depression, and could possibly lead to aggression and other political realignments. It is true that there will be periods of relative stability both in the production and the price of fossil energy. Indeed, there may be periods where brief recessions will cause overproduction and decreasing prices. Nevertheless, I strongly believe that these will be temporary lulls and that, over time, the world is headed in the inevitable direction of a depleting resource, supply volatility, and, therefore, excessive pricing."

The looks of curiosity in his audience had now become visages of fear. Mark felt that he was succeeding in offering a balance to Cavendish's unabashed optimism. Cavendish, however, had remained calm and expressionless.

"In this context, my senior management colleagues and I concluded that Santius needed to stay ahead of the curve and start immediately on a different path. We wanted to align ourselves with alternative energy producers and engage in partnerships with developers to create a new type of vehicle that would no longer be dependent upon the traditional combustion engine, and, therefore, on traditional gasoline energy. I concede this would not be an easy project. On the contrary, it would be a difficult and expensive undertaking that would severely test our excellent team of engineers and our own resolve to succeed. And it would require the patience of our shareholders who would be asked to temporarily park their continued expectations of annual stock appreciation so that we could divert some of our revenues to capital expenditures and our corporate focus into revitalizing your company and to properly position it for the future.

"I believe strongly in the proposed future strategy that I presented to your board of directors. However, I also respect your board's decision to defer its implementation. I believe that Santius's financial viability, indeed its very existence, depends on taking the hard medicine I prescribed. I believe that this new path should be undertaken soon. As importantly, however, I believe without hesitation that our proposed strategy is necessary in order to ensure that Santius's corporate mission statement, 'The company that cares about our environment,' be maintained. I want us to continue to be as proud tomorrow as we were yesterday, that we work for, and invest in, a company that's really trying to make a difference."

Mark sensed the unrest and fear in the audience and decided that it was time for him to make his concluding remarks. "My friends, I also firmly believe in our capitalistic system which, although with its admitted faults, is still the best system we have found. I understand that you, our shareholders, have invested in our company with certain expectations of a reasonable return on your investment. I know there are many investors in this room who are counting on their Santius shares to allow their lifestyles to continue, to let their kids go to college, and to allow them to live their retirement years in self-sufficiency and with personal dignity. I know that asking our shareholders to defer their personal financial interests for three or more years, so that our strategic plan takes hold, is for many too big a sacrifice to endure.

"Since directing this process, I have known from the outset that whether we proceeded with the strategy as proposed, or not, this would be a heart-wrenching exercise for management, for our board, for you the owners, and for me personally. In many ways, in the face of a difficult dilemma, it is always easier and safer to follow the comforts of the status quo instead of venturing into the unknown, whether or not it is ultimately the right decision.

"On your behalf, I want to thank all our employees whose continued loyalty and commitment to Santius are the reasons for its past success. I see many familiar faces in the audience—welcome back. I also see some new friends whom I welcome for the first time. Thank you."

Cavendish was the first to stand, applaud, and shake Mark's hand. The chairman wanted to leave the impression with the shareholders that the two leaders would be united in proceeding with a united strategy that would result in continuing profits for all.

CHAPTER 17

Mark had made no use of his prepared speech punctuated by graphs and charts, quotes from industry experts, specific recommendation details from Merkson, comments from published literature, excerpts from environmentalists, and quotes from OPEC officials.

While Mark never had any intention of pitting Santius's management against its board, he had wanted to make sure that management's full case was squarely placed before the shareholders. He had wanted not so much to contradict the board's decision to reject the proposal, as to indicate that the transition into the new strategy, if not its outright and immediate conversion, should begin soon.

After listening to Cavendish's well-prepared imbroglio, however, Mark had concluded that any deviation from the chairman's stated status quo would have undoubtedly created an internal crisis that would undermine shareholder, customer, supplier, and employee confidence. This, in turn, could lead to unpredictable instability from which Santius might not recover, especially in the context of the present overly competitive environment.

Mark, therefore, decided to instead remain somewhat ambiguous on the expected timing of his proposed strategy and its effects, and, more importantly, on his own future as leader of Santius.

Mark filed his unused written speech into his briefcase and headed toward the throng of media reporters to answer questions and provide additional clarifications. As a true professional, Mark repeated the party line, without straying from Cavendish's commitments, but, at the same time, without adopting them either. While not dejected by the events that had just transpired, Mark felt an inexplicable unease. It was as if he, as much as Burton Cavendish, had engaged in an overt act of misleading Santius, its shareholders, its employees, and most of all, himself, into an untrue perception of his current views and of his future intentions.

"Come on, Mark," Tony whispered to his friend. "I am not letting Marina see you in this condition. You look like you have just seen a ghost. We're going to have a drink, just the two of us, and talk this thing out."

At that particular moment, Mark couldn't think of anyone else with whom he would rather spend the evening. Perhaps rehashing what had just transpired with Tony might help lift the void that Mark now felt in his gut.

CHAPTER 18

Mark felt tired but relieved the following morning. The discussion with Tony the previous evening had helped somewhat. It was like a huge weight had been lifted off his shoulders. Tony had affirmed that Mark had managed not to directly harm Santius by acquiescing to the status quo strategy proposed by Cavendish, while, at the same time, indicating that the company should not, indeed must not, stand still. Tony had seemed confident that Mark had clearly and effectively delivered his prognosis for Santius.

But still, the self-doubt lingered. *Did I say enough to distance myself from Cavendish's self-interested stance of unconditionally leaving things as they are?* Mark thought. *Did I make it clear to the company's shareholders that the switch over to a dramatically different transportation method was not a contestable issue? That, sooner or later, Santius must abandon its current focus and begin the long and admittedly risky journey toward new and unproven technology?* Self-doubt now began to boil over. Mark had always been a person of integrity, uncompromisingly principled, and steadfastly obstinate in pursuing his beliefs.

"I sold my soul to the devil yesterday. I took the easy way out. Cavendish's rejection of my strategy was tantamount to a motion of non-confidence directed at me and my entire management team," Mark said, as Marina sat down to join him for their usual early morning coffee together.

"Mark, you did the right thing yesterday. I followed the meeting online and I saw the reaction of the shareholders. There was relief on their faces when they heard that, while you have firm opinions on the issues, you nevertheless agreed to stay on and lead the company as it transitions into this newer technology." Marina desperately wanted to soothe Mark's inner contradictions. "You had no choice, Mark. Had you abruptly distanced yourself from the board's decision, you would have created a management rift with the board that would have resulted in a crisis in leadership."

Mark looked at Marina lovingly and understood that her comments were primarily intended to appease his self-doubt and stroke his ego.

"I could have said it differently. I could have been more forceful..." his words trailed off to an almost inaudible whisper.

"What's Dior up to today?" Mark asked about his daughter, eager to change topic. Dior was still living at home with her parents, but had plans to move out on her own as soon as she established herself in her job. Marina poured more coffee for both of them. "She's apparently meeting with some friends from her graduating class to talk about how they're going to change the world with their new university degrees. Kids today don't seem to follow the same prescribed paths we did when we graduated. A fulfilling, well-paying job is no longer the sole objective upon graduation. Nowadays, money doesn't matter as much for them. They look for ways to save us from the dangers of an imminent collision between the forces of business and ethics. Things are so difficult now. It all seemed so much clearer and better defined in our time."

Dior was Mark's pride and joy. She had grown up to be a fine young woman with resolve and commitment—a beautiful and gentle woman with clear and decisive ideas. Mark recognized long ago that Dior had her mother's looks and gentle demeanor, but his principles and business savvy. While Mark had been hopeful that Dior would follow his footsteps into Santius or elsewhere in the corporate world, he knew that his daughter's ambitions were much loftier than his, and much less rooted in the need for a financial report card. A smile appeared on Mark's face as he thought about his daughter's future entry into the business world and how she would relish in her ability to balance aggressive business strategies and corporate propriety.

"Give her my love, Marina. Wish her well at her meeting. I want to hear every detail of it this evening. I have a lot to learn from our daughter."

Marina smiled and comforted her husband further. "Dior followed your speech live on the webcast. I am sure the two of you will have plenty to discuss, and plenty to share later this evening."

CHAPTER 19

As Mark eased his car out of the garage that morning, his mind again began to wander back to yesterday's speech. He wondered what impression he had left behind. *Did I come across as an elder statesman with blind loyalty to the company? Or did the shareholders see me as a beaten leader who was conceding defeat to a board chairman who was an unprincipled and grizzled workhorse?* Mark wasn't sure if he had sufficiently buffered himself from the current strategy, which was not only doomed to financial failure, but was unethical because it failed to recognize Santius's wider and more global obligation to the environment.

As Mark accelerated onto the highway ramp toward his office, another troubling thought came to mind: had his speech been an unconscious reflection of his own financial greed? After all, Mark was fifty-seven years old and had been an executive with Santius for much of his business life. While he and his family lived in luxury, and had never seen the need to budget their daily expenses, their lifestyle, incontestably, was costly to maintain. Their expensive home, cars, regular vacations abroad, mountain chalet in Quebec's Mont Tremblant, and luxury beachfront condo in St. Pete Beach—not to mention the latest fashions that filled their closets—were not immodest expenses by any standards.

Mark wondered if he could have done an unconscious analysis of his family's personal balance sheet and concluded that it would be best served, at least in the short-term, by staying the course. *Perhaps,* Mark thought, *I was as self-absorbed in protecting my Santius equity as Cavendish was in protecting his.* Mark had several million share options that would have been negatively impacted by a downward spiral in share value. In fact, his downside was much more substantial than Cavendish's.

Mark reasoned that Cavendish's blatant approach was more laudable then Mark's camouflaged attempt at appearing sanctimonious while, in reality, being anything but altruistic.

As the car purred along the highway, Mark worried about his daughter. *What did Dior think of my comments? Was she proud of me, as she has always been in the past? Or has she now concluded that I've been converted to financial greed?* He was not looking forward to their discussion later in the day, and, ultimately, her verdict.

The office seemed subdued but full of anticipation. Quick smiles of approval and confused glances of uncertainty greeted Mark as he walked down the corridor to his office. "Good morning, boss," Mark was greeted by Jennifer. "Great speech. We're all very proud of you and the way you handled it."

"Good morning, Jen. Thank you. Would you come in to review my appointments for the day?" But before Mark took off his jacket, Tony came in with two coffees, ready for a continuation of their discussion from the previous evening.

Tony had worked with Mark since he'd first joined Santius. He had moved up the corporate ladder steadily over time from marketing manager to vice president of business development. Two years ago, Mark had promoted Tony to executive vice president and chief operating officer. This promotion was a recognition by Mark that no one in the company had a better grasp of the operations and strategies that had made Santius the successful company it had become than Tony.

Tony had a full understanding of what would be needed to ensure Santius's continued viability.

"I've been thinking some more since we spoke last night, Tony. I'm realizing that I didn't seize the opportunity to clearly differentiate between Cavendish's position and mine. I tried to protect the board's party line without ever describing its pitfalls. Worse, I didn't really explain why the strategic position recorded in the consultants' report was the only viable solution to Santius's future predicament."

"Mark, I am telling you that you did all you could. Your speech was the perfect balance between voicing your disagreement with the board's status quo strategy and doing everything possible not to destroy the company through internal acrimony. We all know that had you aggressively touted your strategy, a leadership vacuum would have resulted that would have instantly shaved off a substantial chunk of Santius's market capitalization."

Tony had not only been a loyal colleague, but also, perhaps more importantly, a good friend. A straight shooter, he was a tough-minded operational executive whose real feelings never hid behind platitudes. Mark respected Tony's views and was grateful for his words of support.

"The thing is, Tony, the world has changed forever. The buzz words in the twenty-first century are eco-friendly, fuel-efficiency, climate change, and energy self-sufficiency. This is not just a fading stage like our flower power and peaceniks periods of the sixties. People everywhere are now genuinely concerned about the world we live in, about climate change and global warming, and about the world we'll leave for our children and grandchildren. The concern is genuine. It's real, and it's permanent. There is no turning back."

Mark sipped his coffee. "And it's not just the environment that people are concerned about. It's also about excesses. The old customs of excessively built houses and outrageously priced cars are now entering their golden years. Demographics show that baby boomers are now empty nesters and close to retirement. All of a sudden, the fat expense account is, or will soon be, a thing of the past. The weekly paycheck is gone, the annual bonus has disappeared. The vast majority of these boomers have come to the realization that their retirement has to be funded by their nest eggs—their homes, which are hopefully paid off, and their retirement savings. Surprisingly, they find themselves in a different world. They will have to transition from a lifestyle of free spending funded by regular income and the expense account, to one of careful budgeting. And with the advent of pharmaceutical progress and improving health care, life expectancy has jumped. Some twenty years ago, a seventy-six-year-old male was readying himself for eternal rest. Today, that same person has perhaps another fifteen or more years of an active and expensive lifestyle to fund."

Jennifer interrupted Mark to remind him of his important late afternoon meeting with the manufacturing division managers. After ensuring that it was written on his calendar, Mark continued his thought. "Tony, more and more, people will be worried about excesses. They will worry about overspending on their restricted retirement budgets. And they will worry about the more spiritual and ethical side effects of their prior indulgences, that no one has the singular right to consume more of the earth's material resources than reasonably needed for existence. The big house will be replaced by something more modest, not only to preserve financial security, but also to lower excesses. This means lower maintenance and energy costs, and, generally, a lower social profile."

Tony could almost predict where Mark was going next. "And similarly with cars. People will want eco-friendly and fuel-efficient automobiles more and more. The liberal media, young adults and kids, different levels of government, all will be united in a collective crescendo of opinion that we must, each one of us, do our best to protect the environment by replacing our expensive and depleting fossil fuels with alternative forms of energy that not only preserve the environment, but are also more efficient and therefore less expensive."

Mark's door opened and Jennifer peeked in. "Sorry, Mark, I have to give you this important message." Mark was so totally absorbed in his thoughts that he had not heard her knocking. This was, after all, the whole crux of Mark's corporate strategy.

Jennifer handed Mark a folded note, waited for instructions for a few seconds, but sensing that none would be forthcoming, quietly slipped out of the office and closed the door.

"And on top of everything else, Tony," Mark continued, "the United States government—the government of the largest consumer of traditional energy—has had enough of being taken hostage by OPEC. They are tired of having billions of dollars from grossly inflated oil prices repatriated back to hostile nations with hostile intentions. They are fed up with the prospect that it is indirectly, and perhaps even directly, funding terrorist and other hostile acts directed at the very source of their funding. Talk about biting the hand that feeds you."

Tony had been listening intently and saw his friend almost lost in a reverie. "Mark, you're right. This is why I've supported your initiative right from the start. Time will prove that you're right and that Santius is continuing with its past strategy to its peril. It's a slippery slope. You've persuaded me that the survival of Santius requires a dramatic and risky change in strategy. We have to team up with technology partners that, with our help, will develop commercially viable alternative energy sources. We have seen that electric cars will not fill the need for many years, not until an electric cell is developed that will provide efficiency, distance, and power at a reasonable cost to the consumer."

Mark snapped back, "The answer has to be the development of energy that uses biomass, inedible material, and waste. Tony, the answer lies in biobutanol and cellulosic ethanol, sources that use inedible food waste, wood chips, and other forms of agricultural waste as their main manufacturing components. We need to develop the technology and know-how that will be environmentally friendly and cost-effective. Butanol, for example, is safe, effective, and eco-friendly, and uses redundant food waste and abundant wood particles that can be permanently supplied from the forests of Brazil, Siberia, Asia, Canada, and other parts of the world. The raw technology already exists. Santius simply needs to find the right partner to develop it to commercial scale. Instead of internally funding the development of better car interiors, more supple leathers, and better audio systems, we should be redirecting our focus, and those funds, to develop a cost-efficient source of energy alternatives that will satisfy the need to preserve our environment and make the Western world energy self-sufficient—all in a cost-efficient process."

Mark felt as if he had just sprinted an entire marathon. And just like one of the many marathons he had run in his more youthful years, he had "hit the wall." He was exhausted both physically and mentally. *This*, Mark thought, *is what I wanted to tell Santius's shareholders, that there is an urgent need to switch strategies, that there would be a corporate financial windfall over time, and that this would be accomplished with a strategy that would be good for the environment.* Mark realized that he should have made it clear that he was prepared to continue as CEO of Santius only if the shareholders supported him in this direction.

Mark suddenly became aware of the note that Jen had earlier handed him. He opened it and read: "Burton Cavendish urgently wants to meet you for lunch at Fabrizio's at 1:00 p.m. today." Mark looked at his watch. It was 12:15. If he left now, he would just make it in time.

"Tony, I've gotta go. Thanks for the coffee. And thanks for your support."

As Tony left Mark's office, he smiled. "Heavy luncheon date, I suspect. Good luck."

And with that all-knowing comment, Tony winked at his friend and left the office. Mark grabbed his coat and hurried to his car.

CHAPTER 20

As Mark sped down the freeway for the twenty-five minute drive to Fabrizio's, his mind began analyzing Cavendish's reasons for this unscheduled lunch meeting. While Mark quickly decided that the timing of the recent shareholders' meeting was not mere coincidence and that Cavendish had something important on his agenda to discuss, Mark was unclear on the precise substance and tone of the imminent meeting.

He put pedal to the metal and directed his car toward the restaurant. Both physically and metaphorically, Mark knew that he was headed down a one-way street, with no possibility of detours or U-turns.

Mark's thoughts went back to the discussion he had just had with Tony. This was an issue that needed to be resolved both for the sake of Santius's management, who so deeply believed in the new direction, and for Mark himself, who now, belatedly, saw this issue as the litmus test for his continued leadership of the company. *How can the leader of any business continue to lead indefinitely on a mandate with which he does not agree?* Mark thought. *What would high-principled Dior say about her dad selling out his convictions for a short-term financial gain?*

Mark wondered if he had spent the last thirty-five years of his life building a reputation that could be easily tarnished with a flip-flop in his stance—a stance in which he had, to that point, so unwaveringly believed. He would never allow that to happen. But even with these reassuring thoughts firmed up in his mind, the same nagging thought he had formulated shortly after his speech to the shareholders began to again contaminate his consciousness. *Was I subconsciously evasive in describing my views on the strategic direction of the company in order to fulfill my personal financial goals—as Cavendish did?*

As Mark obsessed over these issues, he concluded that it was perhaps not too late to recapture his lost integrity.

Mark eased his car into Fabrizio's crowded parking lot. The answers to all those thoughts, he felt, were blowing in the wind, to use the lyrics of Peter, Paul and Mary. There would be plenty of time for further analysis—and for answers.

Mark walked into the restaurant with the feeling that he would soon be reaching the proverbial fork in the road. This time, Mark needed to be sure that the path he chose would be clear and firmly followed.

CHAPTER 21

Benvenuto. Welcome back, Signor Gentile," pronounced the affable Fabrizio. "Signora Gentile is well and the bellissima, Dior?"

Fabrizio's was Mark's favorite Italian restaurant and he made a point of regularly holding important meetings there. The food was superb, the atmosphere pure Italian, and Mark cherished the experience each time he dined there. He also looked forward to exchanging a few words in Italian with Fabrizio, often about soccer, their mutual passion. Gently, and at times not so gently, Mark poked fun at Fabrizio's Turin-based Juventus team, and Fabrizio teased Mark about the Inter Milan team. Soccer was a daily obsession for Italians that seemed to define their identity as a people.

Fabrizio's and its jovial owner had become one of Mark's remaining connections to his homeland. Since the death of Mark's parents, it seemed that the traditions, culture, and language of his birthplace had died with them. Fabrizio, it appeared, did his best to build Mark a continuing and active bridge to Italy.

"Buon giorno, Fabrizio. Both Marina and Dior are doing very well. Thank you for asking." Further idle chat was to be postponed for another day. "I'm here to see Burton Cavendish. Has he arrived yet?"

As if Fabrizio sensed that there was a solemnity to this lunch meeting, he quickly led Mark to his favorite corner table at the far end of the smallest of the three dining rooms. From a distance, Mark saw Cavendish and immediately realized that he was sitting in Mark's usual chair. Mark looked at Fabrizio, who turned his face to heaven and put up his hands. "I told him that was your chair, but he wouldn't listen."

As Mark approached, Cavendish stood up and moved forward to greet him.

"Good afternoon, Mark. Please, take a seat," Cavendish said as he offered Mark the chair in which he had been sitting.

"Oh, that's quite all right. I'll sit across from you," Mark said. With his hand on Cavendish's arm, he guided him to sit down. Mark decided that there were more important issues to worry about than Cavendish's desire to play musical chairs and any twisted symbolism that his subtle action might have been intended to convey.

"Thank you for coming on such short notice, Mark. I thought we should have a frank discussion following the events at the shareholders' meeting." *This is a breath of fresh air*, Mark thought. By cutting to the chase, Cavendish bypassed the normally mandatory chat about the health of spouses and dependents, the weather, or the latest sporting event. Mark was in his environment. It was time for him to put his game face on and prepare for what he was now certain would be a quick and decisive battle.

"First, the independent board members met again this morning to review how Santius should proceed in light of the issues raised at the shareholders' meeting. On my personal behalf, and on behalf of the other members, I wanted first to congratulate you on the conciliatory remarks you kindly offered. Any other approach by you would have shaved millions of dollars off Santius's market capitalization."

What an arrogant bastard, thought Mark. *Where did he get the mandate to meet separately with four other board members, to the exclusion of the management board members and without even the courtesy of notice to them? And why does he presume that I, chief executive officer of Santius, need to be patted on the back for not wishing harm on my own company?*

Instead, Mark opted to remain patient and silent.

"I know how difficult it must have been for you to pronounce your agreement with the board's decision for Santius to continue indefinitely with its current strategy—incidentally the same strategy, Mark, that you yourself devised for the company many years ago." At this stage, Mark felt that he could no longer hold back.

But as his thoughts began to take shape, Fabrizio approached their table and, with uncharacteristic timidity, whispered, "Signori, are you ready to order?"

Mark went first. "For me, Fabrizio, simply an insalata Caprese and a bottle of San Pellegrino. For the gentleman—Burt, you don't mind if I order for you, do you?" And without waiting for Cavendish's answer, Mark said, "Pappardelle with salsa di cinghiale." Fabrizio smiled ever so slightly and quickly turned toward the kitchen.

"What did you order for me, Mark? This is your backyard, isn't it? I know this a favorite spot of yours."

Without skipping a beat, Mark replied, "Yes, I do come here quite often. No worries about what I ordered for you. It'll be a pleasant surprise."

Returning to the issue before them, Mark began, "Burt, I did not say that I would agree to indefinitely continue with the status quo. In fact, I said quite the opposite, I believe. I stated that we have the luxury of postponing the implementation of management's proposed strategy only for a short time and only so that we can begin to transition quickly into the development of an alternative energy program and find a technology partner to progress with its development."

Mark settled in his chair and relished the moment. "We need to be less concerned about our immediate financial returns and more thoughtful about doing the right thing for the company and its shareholders. The right thing to do is realize that we are in an industry in aggressive transition and that we must change quickly to meet that challenge. If we are to continue to have an edge over our competitors, we have to understand that the financial rewards will come later as a result of the mandate that we decide to pursue now. The days of fossil fuel are numbered. We must move into the area of creating eco-friendly, replenishing, and efficient energy to power our cars. Cellulosic ethanol, biobutanol, hydrogen, electric—"

"Here is the pappardelle al cinghiale. Homemade pasta in a, what you call it, pig ragu?"

Mark immediately corrected Fabrizio. "Wild boar ragu."

"This wild boar ragu sauce, you will enjoy," Fabrizio added, half maliciously. "This homemade specialty has, how you say it, your name on it, Mr. Cavendish. It was prepared by our kitchen, especially for you."

As Cavendish pondered whether this was Mark's subtle reprisal for the chair incident or merely Fabrizio's effusiveness, Mark continued. "Santius is not a personal holding company. It was not intended to create personal advantages for any one person or for any one special segment of shareholders. It was not founded to quickly repair any past financial misfortunes caused by previous negative investments. Santius is, and was intended to be, an opportunity for all shareholders, regardless of personal circumstances.

"We must do what is right for the company. If we stay true to that simple rule, everything else will resolve itself automatically. And what is right for Santius is that we immediately heed the findings of the retained experts and the strong recommendations of my management team. Santius must convert over to the new strategy, and it must do so soon, before it's too late."

While Mark had attempted to make it seem that his speech was not directed to any one person in particular, he was sure that it was clear to Cavendish that he had thoroughly researched his past.

"Mark, this is really the crux of why I wanted to meet with you privately today. The independent directors strongly believe that for the benefit of Santius, you ought to clarify to the public that, at least for the next three to five years, this risky venture you have advocated will be deferred and that Santius will concentrate on continuing to make fuel-efficient vehicles as it has in the past. After all, we're not running out of fossil fuels immediately. There are known and potential deposits that will see uninterrupted supplies for the next fifty years or more. Nor is there any hard evidence that, over the long haul, the price of the commodity will continue to rise in the same dramatic way as in the last couple of years. The Middle East oil sheikhs have all been educated in economics at Oxford, Harvard, and Yale. They know and understand that a devastating global recession would result from any long-term manipulation of the supply of oil. Hell, where do you think these people invest their profits? Right back into North America and Western Europe. They can't afford to cripple our Western industries because to do so would be to deal a deathblow to their own profits."

Cavendish added, "It wouldn't surprise me one bit if the oil barons in fact owned a large stake in Santius."

Mark recognized that Cavendish was eloquently summarizing the contrary position and that, in the end, there was no evidentiary way to determine today who was right and who was wrong.

"And as to the need for this so called eco-friendly energy…hell, Mark, I have been on this earth a good many years. I have seen fads like this come and go. Brigitte Bardot and her campaign to protect the seals, hippie types with their flower power in the sixties and seventies, and more recently, Al Gore preaching environmental calamity, the melting of the ice caps, the march of the penguins, and eventually Armageddon if we don't jog or ride our bikes to work or turn down the heat in our homes by a degree or two."

Mark saw that Cavendish was warming up for his finale.

"What these geniuses fail to understand is the basic principle that guides our existence. Nature has a built-in balance of forces that will destroy and replenish precisely in order to keep a harmonious balance. Humans are part of this natural balance. We should stay out of it and not interfere. By some estimates, our good earth has existed for over four billion years and has developed and evolved very nicely without human interference. It will go on for another four billion years, so long as we don't feel that we know best and try to interfere with the forces of nature."

With altruistic philosophizing transparently camouflaging blatant financial greed, Cavendish continued. "We can't stop progress, Mark, and we can't stop man's ambition to better his lot in life. Making a profit isn't a bad thing. Having a decent return on one's investment is not objectionable. People have placed their hard-earned money in Santius, expecting profit maybe to pay off a mortgage, a car loan, or a dependent's college tuition, or to fund retirement. You may describe these objectives as greed. I don't. I see these as laudable personal objectives that define everyday life. We don't know whether any one investor in Santius expects a return today or tomorrow. We need to direct Santius toward a path of continuity rather than engaging in your professed immediate change that dramatically and immediately impacts profitability."

Unquestionably, Cavendish's words were thoughtful and biting. And while Mark immediately saw the faultiness of his reasoning, there could be no doubt that Cavendish, as if to validate his theory of natural balance, had put forward an eloquent rebuttal to Mark's position.

Cavendish cut into his wild boar. "Mark, what I am about to say is very difficult for me." He paused a moment for effect and then stated emphatically, "We want you to immediately make a public statement, through a press release, to the effect that you intend to continue to lead Santius as in the past and will pursue its current strategy indefinitely. If you wish, you may add some innocuous color to the effect that you and your management team will continue to look at opportunities to improve Santius's corporate objectives as they may arise. The majority of the board has concluded, however, that it's essential for you to make a clear and unequivocal statement at this time to ensure that there is no confusion as to the continuing direction of our company. I am therefore directing you to have a draft of a press release for my review early tomorrow morning so that the company's disclosure committee can consider it for the full board's review and approval. I want this statement to be on the wires tomorrow evening after close of the markets."

Mark was stunned by the direct harshness of Cavendish's words. He did not react outwardly, but his emotions were in turbulence. His professionalism and his experience compelled him to make a parting comment. "Burt, I'll carefully consider your comments and I will have a draft release for you in the morning."

Mark sat back in his chair and smiled. "Now, allow me to order dessert for both of us."

"If your choice of dessert is as good as the boar, I'm in for a treat," Cavendish said. Mark couldn't help but notice Cavendish's ironic smile.

CHAPTER 22

Inexplicably, the exchange with Cavendish had left Mark invigorated physically, and at peace mentally.

As he aimed his car toward the freeway for his evening journey home, Mark felt the exhilaration of a sinner who had been thrown a lifeline. Ever since his statement at the shareholders' meeting, Mark had felt as if he had been living in ambiguity. He had taken refuge under carefully chosen semantics that had been intended to conceal his personal views. Had he been true to his principles, Mark would have clearly declared that Santius either needed to be transformed with him at the helm or that it would languish in the status quo under the leadership of Admiral Cavendish. Instead, Mark had sacrificed his integrity. He had sold his soul to the devil, as it were.

As the melodic harmony of Puccini's aria softly wafted through the car's cabin, Mark concluded that, unbeknownst to Cavendish, his directive had provided Mark with an opportunity for his redemption. Would he seize it this time or slip back into paralysis? Would Mark once again compromise his principles?

Mark pulled into his driveway. When he opened the front door and stepped inside, he knew there was no turning back. He closed the door behind him. His past had been metaphorically sealed and nothing would ever be the same.

PART II

Probing the soul
In a distant land.
Searching for the undefinable.
No clear path,
An unknown destination.
The experiences of a
Distant youth,
The generosity of a people
Uncover
Internal turmoil,
And the ability to quell it.

CHAPTER 23

At 35,000 feet, Mark felt serene and at peace with himself. With the stroke of a pen, he had ended his days of internal turmoil.

Burt,

In light of our recent discussions, it has become clear to me that my personal vision for the continued growth and excellence of Santius is not shared by you and a majority of the board of directors. Rather than engage in an internal dissenting process that would be severely harmful to our valued employees and will undoubtedly have negative repercussions for our customers, suppliers, and advisers, I have decided that the least prejudicial course of action is for me to resign from my position as chief executive officer. In order that Santius be able to focus on planning for my successor at the earliest, I am advising you that my resignation is effective immediately.

Best,
Mark

Mark smiled as he played those magical last words in his mind: "…my resignation is effective immediately." He had acted swiftly and decisively, without rancor, and, importantly, without personal ill will toward Cavendish. He felt especially pleased for not being vindictive, something that might have well been excused under the circumstances.

Mark settled into his plane seat and looked out the window. He felt a calmness he had not felt for a long time. "Effective immediately." Those words had resonated with Marina and Dior the evening after lunch at Fabrizio's, when he told them of his encounter with Cavendish and of the decision he had reached. Mark knew that a principal reason why he felt so positive about his decision was the unconditional familial support he knew he would receive from his wife and daughter.

"Dad, I'm really proud of you," Dior had said. "As I start my own career, I've been thinking about how I hope I can live by the same code of morality and integrity you've shown. I hope I never favor personal ambition or material wealth over virtues."

That evening, Mark had floated to his family the idea of him taking considerable time off to reconnect with his emotions, to purge himself of these latest experiences, and to determine for himself whether the old sets of socially imposed values were still relevant to him. As expected, Mark's proposed self-discovery was received enthusiastically by both Marina and Dior. They recognized that he needed to engage in that process, that he needed to do it quickly, and, most of all, that he needed to do it alone.

It was not with much surprise that Mark's refuge for his personal quest for self-discovery was none other than his birthplace.

Mark had considered, but quickly disregarded, fancy executive spas, Caribbean resorts, Arizona mountain retreats, and Wyoming ranches—the usual destinations for malcontents and overstressed executives. Instead, he had been pulled to his roots. He sought the serenity of the simple life that Acerenza offered.

Yes, his personal reevaluation would take place at 19 Via Sileo— the small house with two-feet-thick stone walls that had been passed through the Gentile generations and was a site of happy childhood memories for Mark.

As Mark sipped from his glass of pinot grigio, the gentle murmur of the aircraft's powerful engines began to slowly relax him and blunt his consciousness. Soon, he was magically transported back to a happier time and place; to a tranquil, pastoral-like scene where he, a very young Marco, walked hand-in-hand with his aging grandfather through the family vineyards, ripe with fruit. They inspected the vines here and there, smelling and living the remnants of autumn's glory as the sun's golden rays provided the last nourishment to nature's bounty.

Mark reflected on his daily sprint from school to Alvanello, and other incidents in his distant youth. He wondered when things had become so much more complicated. *Will I ever be able to recapture the balances in life that, along the way, seem to have become lost?* Mark asked himself. *Can I experience the simplicities of yesteryear and recapture my youthful ideals? Will I ever be able to find Marco?*

Through the darkness, somewhere over the Atlantic Ocean, Mark began to discern a distant glow on the eastern horizon. "My adventure awaits just beyond," he whispered to himself with deep satisfaction.

CHAPTER 24

Rome's Leonardo da Vinci airport was, as usual, chaotic on Mark's arrival. A cacophony of voices—Italian and foreign—battled one another to be heard. Children screamed in delight as their flying adventures began—or ended. Adults yelled as they tried to wade through the throngs of hurried passengers. The airport was filled with an organized confusion of sound and movement that shocked the senses and energized the body.

Mark felt exuberant and inexplicably happy and carefree. He was in his homeland and about to reconnect with his roots in a time of personal need. After so many years of striving for business goals that seemed so crucial at the time, Mark now sensed, in the middle of this organized Italian chaos, that his past successes had not really fulfilled him in life's most important objective: the awareness of one's true character and the satisfaction of knowing that one was leading a balanced life.

As Mark, baggage in hand, attempted to navigate through the crowds in the arrival area, his temples began to flush at the thought that he was only coming to this realization now, after decades of striving in a world that seemed to recognize only material successes, and rewarded such successes with dollars, rather than self-satisfaction.

As Mark hailed a taxi to Stazione Termini, where his train to Acerenza was waiting, he had the nagging thought that he was about to begin a reevaluation of his past life. He felt that, somehow, Mark the teacher would give Mark the student of life a failing grade. It seemed that his life was about to take a dramatically different turn, with an unclear path and an unknown destination.

But Mark's final encounter with Cavendish had spurred him to this life reassessment, and he knew there was no turning back. He was excited by that prospect. Cavendish now seemed to be quickly fading in his rearview mirror. His life at Santius felt like a dated movie reel that belonged to a different era with a different reality. Mark was amazed at how quickly he had extinguished from his mind what had been such an important part of his life for so many years.

As the taxi wound its way to the railway station, Mark tapped the driver on his shoulder. "Fermati un istante, per piacere" (Stop a moment, please). The driver pulled over to the side and Mark stepped out of the cab and disappeared into a cafe. He reemerged a moment later with an impeccably dressed server in tow with two cups of espresso—one for himself and the other for the cab driver. "Grazie tanto, signore," offered the driver.

"Salute," replied Mark, as they clinked their espresso cups.

There's no better way to celebrate my arrival in my homeland, thought Mark as they headed to the train station.

CHAPTER 25

The train station of any city in Italy is a microcosm of that city's very existence. Stazione Termini was no exception. It had a living, breathing pulse. It was a display of life itself. It was on its stage that the everyday dramas of life were performed and where the best and the worst of the Italian character and temperament collided endlessly on both important and meaningless activities.

As Mark walked through the station, he noticed with fascination how queuing for anything, from buying a *panino* on the go to purchasing train tickets, was a habit reserved largely for the too-polite English, Japanese, and North Americans; the Italians didn't have time to queue for services. They needed to get these details behind them as quickly as possible so that they could walk over to the nearest café and spend countless hours, cappuccino in hand, commiserating life in general and blasting away at the current Italian political landscape in particular, with their newest best friend sitting next to them.

Mark witnessed expressions of effusiveness, anger, generosity, tolerance, and impatience—all intrinsically woven together—occur in one or several unrelated incidents, by one person or many. All the Italian women Mark knew had the passion and independence of Sofia Loren in everything they did. And all the Italian men he'd met were fiercely aggressive on a soccer pitch, yet became lame and subservient in the company of their female companions. Italy was dominated by women who dictated how human relationships were carried out.

Italy's effervescent prime minister, Silvio Berlusconi, may have had political and financial clout, but Mark, and every Italian, knew who dominated the relationship between the head of state and his wife. Who, in Italy, could ever forget Berlusconi's forced public apology to his wife? His inappropriate but harmless comment about a young female member of his cabinet drew the ire of an entire nation, men and women alike—although, Mark suspected, with conflicting personal emotions on the part of the males. There was no option for Berlusconi, even as the most powerful and influential man in the country—and, perhaps, especially so for this reason—but to swallow his ego and succumb to the dais with a public apology carried on all of Italy's media as the principal news item. All other world events—the Afghanistan crises, China's drive toward economic supremacy—took a secondary role to this conflict of the heart.

Women in Italy have always been placed on a pedestal by their adoring male counterparts; Italian men wouldn't have it any other way. Mark needed only to listen to the romantic lyrics of Italian songs—especially Neapolitan love ballads that invariably pulled at the very heartstrings of human emotion—to understand this.

Jealousy was a human emotion pervading the sunny peninsula; men and women alike seemed to equally suffer from the phenomenon. And so, even a stranger's quick gaze at a man's girlfriend could provoke antagonism in the man—directed not at the stranger but at his companion herself. And heaven forbid a man rested his eyes, even for an instant, on another signorina! Such was an unforgiveable sin punished by a variety of reactions: screams, violent body language intended to embarrass the companion, public and private temper tantrums, and, if all else failed to accomplish the objective of conscious and visible retribution, tears. Not simply wetness by the corner of the eye, but a veritable flood.

These were not private encounters, as decency would require. In Italy, they were often very public demonstrations—and were intended to be. Each side pleaded their case as if before a judicial officer—often inviting, by conduct or words, bystanders to take sides. It was a participatory process. Every Italian lover—whether smitten or accusatory—was trained in the advocacy of emotionally-driven superlatives and hyperbole. Italian adversaries were at once the victim, the lawyer, the judge, and the jury.

Mark remembered an encounter between Giovanni and Silvana, two Italian friends. For three days following a misdirected glance or two by Giovanni, Silvana treated Giovanni, alternately, with disdain and indifference. On the fourth day, however, the meting out of punishment on Giovanni was deemed to have run its course, and Silvana converted her demeanor from neglect to pity for her tempted weak lover. Giovanni seized the opportunity to profess his undying love for Silvana, and with his own tears mingling with hers, they embraced and declared that the unfortunate incident was behind them forever, never to recur…until a few days later, when temptation again seized Giovanni and the curtain rose for Act II.

What actors, these Italians! thought Mark. *What wonderful, energetic, eloquent, emotional, loving, and caring actors.* There were no understudies in Italy; only principal performers in their prime, conducting life's drama through the many vagaries of the heart. There was no fakery; only deeply held emotions straight from *l'anima* (the soul). Dante's Divine Comedy did not do justice to Silvana's melodrama.

As Mark boarded the train to Acerenza, he felt a deep sense of satisfaction and pride that he was a member—admittedly only by birth—of a people who in the past have not only given so much to the world through their art, science, music, fashion, culture, and literature, but who made love and its uninhibited outward expression part of their daily existence.

CHAPTER 26

Progress had been slow in Acerenza compared to the more affluent parts of Italy. The town and its neighbors seemed to have been forgotten by the modern world, and had, happily, not yet been discovered by the digital camera-laden Germans, Brits, Japanese, and North Americans. Its isolation was partly due to the one road that connected the railway station in the valley to the rest of the area. The road traveled past the lazy waters of the River Bradano, and then climbed up vertiginously past vineyards clinging to the mountainside, sloping wheat fields, fruit orchards, and a million kinds of multicolored wild flowers.

As the train approached the outskirts of town, Mark saw the most obvious result of modern-day progress: Acerenza now had a suburb, of sorts. Newer edifices had sprung up in the lower flat land, below the ancient town, to house the new generation of Acerenzesi—or what's left of them. The older folks continued to live inside the gates of San Canio. Anyone outside the gates was once considered not to be a "true" Acerenzese. And so, a gentle but clear dichotomy began to develop between the two groups, though only in jest. Mark noticed that the massive ancient gates that the Acerenzesi had at one time used to lock up the village every night—to keep away the variety of thieves, criminals, and malcontents whose role in life was to go from town to town to steal and pillage—now remained open.

As the train neared the station in Acerenza, Mark's childhood memories—subconscious memories that he had rarely had the time to consider before now—flowed back. These memories had been relegated to the deepest recesses of his mind so that sufficient room could be cleared for his law degrees, his career ambitions, his family, and his busy life in general.

Although Mark's memories went back a half a century in time, and were formed during a relatively miniscule time frame, nevertheless, they now pervaded his entire being. Mark's Italian double, Marco, was now a prisoner of his own mind. Small incidents that had occurred a lifetime ago now took shape and were lovingly visualized in every minute detail.

◆

"Marco, tonight when it is dark, we climb our neighbor's cherry tree and pick cherries," little Marco's grandfather whispered. "Their cherries are better than ours, but we have better hazelnuts and figs. We have a silent agreement with our neighbor—we pick their cherries and they repay themselves with our figs and hazelnuts." The old man said this to no one in particular, but he felt the need to explain and justify to his grandson their covert action.

And so, the conspiracy between Marco and his grandfather was complete. As day turned into night and the bright moon chased away the sun, the two thieves, disparate in size but with a common objective, headed to the neighboring property, hand-in-hand, with nothing but the moon as an approving witness to their forthcoming furtive deed.

Marco treasured these nights on their farm, when he and his grandfather were alone to enjoy each other's company. And these evenings, soundless except for the chorus of cicadas celebrating the end of another day, began after twilight, as Nonno told stories in front of the open hearth, with the glowing embers providing warmth, light, comfort, and security. No matter how benevolent the story his grandfather told, there was always a twist involving some misadventure that captivated Marco and allowed him to drift off to a sound sleep while attempting to unravel the twisted plot.

And so it was with Marco and his grandfather. It was a special and undying bond that continued unabated until Nonno was taken away from Marco many years later.

CHAPTER 27

Mark's reverie was shaken by the screeching of metal as the two-car train pulled into the Acerenza station. Rome's Stazione Termini was now a world away. Gone was the helter-skelter of activities driven by hordes pulling and pushing in different directions. Rather, a tranquility had set in. Only a few passengers struggled out of the train with bags or children in hand. Time stood still. Schedules appeared irrelevant.

Mark looked over toward the valley, the river meandering through it, and up the mountainside, and was instantly enveloped by a sense of calmness and nostalgia. He had returned to his native roots. Still, there was anxiety in his heart. Would he feel like he still belonged, decades later? Or would he feel like a stranger to a place abandoned by him except for one short visit some twenty years earlier? Indeed, Mark's return to his native town was not simply out of sentimentality. He had an inner burden to resolve.

For now, though, he became mesmerized by the indescribable beauty all around him. Basilicata in late September was at its most beautiful, and Acerenza, in particular, sparkled with color in a way that neither a poet with words nor an artist with canvas could ever do it justice. As the bus Mark had boarded crossed the river for its long trek up the mountain, Mark's eyes were transfixed on the scenes all around him. Vineyards with endless rows of vines almost ready to bear fruit could be seen in perfect symmetry. Olive groves and orchards of apples, hazelnuts, walnuts, and figs appeared and disappeared with every twist and turn of the road. Wheat fields, recently harvested, glowed in the sunlight, resting for next year. Wildflowers displayed hues that Mark could never have imagined.

Why had he not seen these wonders before now? Why had he not sensed this natural beauty earlier in life? *Is this heaven?* thought Mark. *Or am I finally seeing a heaven that has been here all along but kept itself secluded from my senses?*

The constant climb up the mountain caused many of the bus passengers to doze off, but Mark was anything but sleepy. His feelings were tingling, his mind was alert, and his emotions were flowing. Mark felt, at that moment, like he could never sleep again, for fear that this dream would abruptly end and he would be transported back in time to his life on executive lane.

Mark's thoughts drifted to Alvanello, the vineyard that his grandfather has passed on to him. He had received sporadic annual reports from Marcello, the vineyard's caretaker, on the state of the vineyards and the olive groves, but few decisions had needed to be made over the years. The grapes and olives were harvested annually and were sold to cooperatives that, in turn, converted them to juice and oil respectively. The co-ops then sold these to various wholesalers who produced wine and olive oil and branded them for ultimate sale through distributors.

Mark's bus pulled into the center of town. A quick glance at the sides of Acerenza's simple square—Piazza Centrale—revealed the vaguely recognizable post office building; the neighboring variety store where Mark's mother used to buy him treats; Budini's Caffè next to it, owned by the parents of Mark's childhood best friend, Gianni; and one of the two old barber shops in town, now converted into a jewelry store. After stepping off the bus, Mark walked across the square toward the lane that would lead to the home where he had been born. Since the passing of Mark's grandfather, the house at 19 Via Sileo had been regularly used as a family retreat by Mark's Italian cousins to escape the stifling Roman summers. Although the house, the vineyards, and the farm had devolved upon Mark, he had not been back for many years. Nevertheless, by instinct and an indelible recollection, he walked assuredly on the uneven cobblestone street on which no automobile had ever passed. It was a small street that, for many hundreds of years, had been frequented by playful children; women doing their daily tasks and who were never too busy to say a few words to anyone and everyone who walked by; and men dragging donkeys and mules carrying chests laden with fruits and vegetables.

Mark was transported back in time. As he opened the door to his native home, it was as if his very soul had been unlocked. For a moment, he stood there seemingly paralyzed by the flowing sentiments of yesteryear. The memory of his grandparents welcomed him back home.

The house was a two-story building, narrow but deep. The main floor had remained virtually intact, unaffected by technology and progress. The large fireplace, smaller than Mark remembered, was the focal point of the first level. Mark spent many evenings in front of the hearth, munching on roasted chestnuts and fire-grilled focaccia while his grandfather regaled him with adventure stories.

The antique dining table and straw chairs were exactly as they had been when Mark was a child. *If only these objects could talk*, Mark thought. *Oh, the stories they could tell and the happiness during festive and special occasions they could describe.*

The only signs of modern times Mark noticed were a small gas-fired stove next to the fireplace—no doubt to complement, rather than replace, the hearth—and a newly tiled sink with running water. When Mark was a child, water was still fetched from communal fountains fed by natural mountain springs. At the far end of the small room, was a flush-toilet—another relatively new "invention" for 19 Via Sileo.

Mark moved upstairs. From his second floor bedroom, he stared at the rooftops and beyond, toward the mountains in the distance.

Vivid memories of his childhood flashed back. He felt as if he were a child again, transported to what was a carefree and happy time.

◆

Little Marco liked to peer at the distant line of mountains through the balcony window and dream of faraway lands.

One day, he sat on his grandfather's horse as it obediently wound its way first down the valley and then up the steep climb to one of the neighboring towns. Marco sat as erect and proud as could be, his eyes twinkling as the excitement of adventure pervaded his mind.

The next day, little Marco's imagination created an adult Marco, mature and important, with a briefcase full of complex papers and documents neatly tucked into a file folder that rested on the passenger seat of his gleaming new Lancia automobile. As Marco, the business tycoon, negotiated the hairpin turns away from Acerenza toward his business destination, little Marco's hyperactive imagination visualized conflicts and negotiations that would ultimately lead to successful conclusions.

These adventures usually ended with the repeated call of his mother to come downstairs at once and get ready for dinner.

◆

During that imaginary period, Marco was in another place, happier than the one in which Mark had played his executive roles. Although every decision he had taken at Santius had seemed at the time to have been important to him and crucial to the company's development, they were all so insignificant now. For the first time, he began to feel that, perhaps, the rewards to which he had been accustomed might not have been the true measure of his performance in life. What was the right reward? It was this question, more than any other, that Mark was now silently asking himself. He had come to Acerenza to uncover its answer.

Mark had been pulled back to his roots inexplicably. There was no agenda, no expectations, no time frame, and no personal pressure to uncover life's secrets or the key to personal happiness. No, this was merely a personal quest intended to rationalize Mark's professional life to that point and to determine the right path for him to follow in the future. The road to conclusion lay not in global adventures, but, rather, in accessing the soul—that indefinable hub of emotions, rationalizations, intelligence, ethics, and other characteristics that make up every person's "being."

As these daunting thoughts permeated his mind, Mark felt at ease with himself. He felt as if the guidance he was seeking could only be sourced in Acerenza's mellow sunrises and sunsets; in the smells and sounds of the traditional grape and olive harvests; in the honest daily activities of the gentle and hard-working people; and in the memories that he had forever trapped in his mind, but long neglected.

CHAPTER 28

When Mark opened his eyes from his prolonged sleep, the sun was already high in the blue sky. It was a minute before he was sufficiently conscious enough to hear faint knocking at the front door. Throwing back the covers, Mark jumped out of bed, hurried down the stairs, and opened the door.

"Buon giorno, Marco," the excited man said. "Marco Gentile," he continued, "you don't remember me? I am Luca, Luca Moranni. Your friend from when we were this high." The man motioned to a height near his hip.

"Of course I remember you, Luca!" Mark said. "Come in, come in."

Mark, Luca, and a third friend, Gianni, were known in town as the Tre Moschettieri. They were inseparable, full of adventure, and always on the verge of getting in trouble. "Trouble" in those days meant "borrowing" from the abundant farms—an apple here, some grapes there, a pomegranate, some figs—not because they were in need of nature's gifts (both Mark and Luca had their respective family farms for a ready supply), but because the danger of taking these fruits without permission filled them with an indescribable sense of adventure. The farm owners were "in" on this game, and so they would alternately yell at them, chase them away, or threaten to put their vicious dog on their tail—all the while suppressing a smile of understanding, an understanding that these activities were the stuff that evolved children into adults. It was purely an exciting game, never tainted by risk or danger.

"Marco, the fun we had. The trouble we got into, you, Gianni, and me. We were a dangerous team. We were 'I tre Briganti,' pirates—"

"Moschettieri, not briganti. Moschettieri. But yes, we were a dangerous trio," agreed Mark with a smile. The two friends embraced. Mark felt their common childhood memories and fantasies come flooding back.

The two friends sat at the dining table, and then, in a rapid exchange, Luca caught Mark up on everything that had happened since he'd left.

"Gianni and his parents moved to Belgium shortly following your departure for America, and left Budini's Caffè in the hands of Amelia." Amelia was Gianni's sister. "At first, Gianni and his parents returned to Acerenza every year for a few days at Christmas, but then, as time passed, their visits became more sporadic," Luca said. "I haven't seen Gianni for many years, but Amelia told me that he's now married with three children and living in Brussels where he operates a small but successful trattoria.

"I, on the other hand, have never left Acerenza. I married Anna, the most beautiful woman in town, and we have two wonderful children who now work and live in Ravello. I'm also the police chief of Acerenza—a position of much importance and influence," Luca was quick to add.

It mattered little that Acerenza was a small, law-abiding town where the biggest crime that Luca was called upon to settle was an argument between two neighbors about the noise of the other's dog barking in the middle of the afternoon, thus disturbing the *riposo dopopranzo* (afternoon nap). Nor did it matter that as "chief," Luca had no subordinates. He was a one-man police force, although clearly loved and respected by the entire Acerenza citizenry.

Luca insisted on giving his friend a personal tour of the new Acerenza, so that he could see for himself the progress that had been made since his departure for America.

Luca rose up and proudly announced, "America is not the only place of progress. Here in Acerenza, we also have big screen televisions, mobile phones, and cars, cars everywhere. Even one or two Mercedes."

How ironic, thought Mark. *Luca wishes to elevate Acerenza's progress into the twenty-first century at the very time I'm looking to return to a simpler place.*

Mark mused that perhaps his friend's descriptions had been propelled by personal pride, rather than by reality, as a way of ensuring that Mark knew that Luca had given up nothing by way of lifestyle by deciding voluntarily to remain in Acerenza and make his life there.

The official town tour commenced with much fanfare, as Luca began their rounds. "This is the same Marco who was born in Acerenza and who was forced to immigrate against his will to America where he has distinguished himself by becoming a true American big shot," Luca said to everyone they met. At times, there would be a sign of recognition. On those occasions, the handshake would be firmer or the embrace tighter and more prolonged as the townsperson would briefly recount an ancient story about Mark's parents or grandparents.

Except for Mark's godfather, Father Leo, one of two long-retired town priests who still lived in Acerenza, Mark's entire family line no longer had any presence in town. But people still remembered them. The older men recounted their personal experiences with Mark's grandfather. The women looked skyward and, while crossing themselves, declared that Mark's grandmother and mother were both saints sitting in heaven as their just reward for having led such honest and spiritual lives—and for having raised such a fine and virtuous young man.

And so it went for several hours. Luca made certain that Mark's arrival in Acerenza was known throughout the town so that everyone could greet and welcome him back, especially as a sign of respect for his parents and grandparents.

Mark was genuinely moved by the townspeople's sincere affection, loving simplicity, and good wishes toward a person, who, for many years, had been a forgotten Acerenzese. They expected nothing in return for their warm welcome, except mutual friendship and a recognition that, as humans destined to live together on this planet, we should celebrate social encounters without precondition. Wealth, achievements, and community standing did not matter in Acerenza. What was important was the integrity with which one undertook his daily actions or omissions. To these people, the measure of one's stature in life was determined by the respect that had been earned, not by one or even several acts, but by a lifetime of constant and continuous virtue.

This, Mark concluded, was indeed the right environment for him in which to take measure of his own life and make the required changes for the future.

CHAPTER 29

Fatigue from the long trip and Mark's emotions began to take over. It took all of his remaining energy to detach himself from Luca, who was ready to stick close to his friend for the entire evening.

"First we have a nice espresso at Budini's, and then we have dinner, the best rabbit stew with homemade gnocchi that you ever tasted, Marco," said Luca excitedly. "And then we go to the Dopolavoro Bar for a game of billiards and a grappa." While Luca reluctantly accepted his friend's fatigue as a sufficiently good reason to skip dinner and after-dinner drinks, nevertheless, he insisted on visiting the nearby Budini's for coffee.

The consumption of food is an important rite in Italian life. It is not simply a matter of ingesting energy to survive; it is an occasion used to celebrate life itself. The simplest meal becomes an essential experience. The *primo piatto* (appetizer) is followed by a *secondo*, and then perhaps a cheese plate with a green salad to clear the palate for *il dolce* (dessert). This is followed by *il caffè*. No meal is ever eaten in a hurry. Food and drink are to be cherished, savored—never inhaled by osmosis, as is often the custom in North America. The meal is almost an excuse, a delicious and extraordinary justification, to partake in conversation with friends or family. It is at the dinner table that Italy's most important issues—politics, love, romance, and *calcio* (football)—are debated for hours. Debates can go from being lively to drawing out the deepest passions of the soul.

Mark thought that Italians were at their best during discussions over food. *Their body language, gesticulations, and eloquent speech all rise to new levels of articulation. In Italy, there is more respect for form articulated with passion than the deepest substance blurted out without gusto. It seems that everyone here is a Mark Antony or a Luigi Pirandello or a Dante Alighieri*, Mark thought.

Mark could still recite by heart Dante's famous lines from the introduction to his long journey to the Inferno—lines Mark had memorized in a literature course an eternity ago:

> *Nel mezzo del cammin di nostra vita*
> *mi ritrovai per una selva oscura,*
> *ché la diritta via era smarrita.*

> *[Midway through the passage of life's journey*
> *I found myself in a dark forest,*
> *Where the right path was lost.]*

Mark's mental meanderings were abruptly interrupted by Luca.

"You want sugar in your espresso, Marco?" asked Luca as he arrived at their table in Budini's with two small espresso cups. The two old friends lingered over the cups for a long time.

After they had finished their drinks, Mark affectionately thanked his friend for the tour of town, and alleviated Luca's heartfelt disappointment at his early withdrawal by promising that they would be having many dinners and many days together during his prolonged stay in Acerenza.

Mark walked through the deserted cobblestone streets, the silence broken now and again by a passerby offering a "buona sera," or by the sound of a television program wafting through an open door.

Nel mezzo del cammin di nostra vita, thought Mark. Just as Dante, in his midlife, had embarked on a journey to discover the essence of spirituality, so too had Mark begun his personal odyssey to find his true identity and awaken his soul to spirituality. Unlike Dante, however, there would be no exciting adventures in Mark's personal inner travels. Mark would be the principal and sole actor in this private screening and the only tools at his disposal would be the inspiration drawn from his hometown and its hospitable citizenry, the power of his own reflection, and the honesty of his own convictions.

"*...Mi ritrovai per una selva oscura, ché la diritta via era smarrita...*" Mark believed that the darkness described by Dante was much like the diminished integrity he had felt when Cavendish had asked him to compromise his principles in favor of an immediate fix driven largely by personal greed. It had been a wake-up call for Mark. Could he shape his life in a way that corporate exigencies could live harmoniously and in balance with other important values in life, such as integrity, honesty, and unconditional self-fulfillment?

There would, indeed, be much to consider, but a sudden visit from Morpheus meant that further reflection would have to wait for another day.

CHAPTER 30

Mark slept for ten straight hours, twice his usual nightly average. He was awakened by the clatter of hoofs on the cobblestones and excited voices in the street below. The day had long since begun to take shape in Acerenza.

A procession of mules and donkeys strapped with chests laden with figs, olives, grapes, chestnuts, and a rainbow of vegetables filed past. These precious items would be emptied into smaller straw containers which would then be strategically placed outside the farmer's door, for sale to those whose career paths did not include toiling the good earth. There would be no sticker price on these products. The "consideration" (the term Mark had been in the custom of using during his executive tenure), or the price, would always be a matter of quick and friendly negotiation between vendor and purchaser, often, at the buyer's discretion. There would never be a failed sale because of price. Hence, no need to worry about *caveat emptor*. The sole criterion for an immediate acquisition would be the buyer's need. Nor was there ever an issue with the products' quality. The reputation and personal integrity of the farmer would ensure that only the finest of his products would be offered to his compatriots. A too ripe tomato or a fig that hadn't met the owner's own expectations would be sifted out and appropriated for personal consumption rather than sale to a neighbor. To offer such diminished quality would be a crime—no, worse, it would be a sin. It could never be allowed.

The business world could learn a very valuable lesson here, thought Mark while lying in bed. Rather than squeezing out every penny of profit margin that a business could get away with, the guiding principle here was one of selling and buying a quality product at a fair price. No need for handsomely paid attorneys to interpret some ambiguous contractual obligation. In this environment, time dockets and monthly legal accounts had been replaced by personal satisfaction, reputation, and integrity. And the system, in its full simplicity, had worked well for many centuries.

Mark soon got out of bed and dressed before leaving the house. As he walked along Via Sileo toward Budini's Caffè in the piazza, he felt happy and at ease with himself. He had rarely thought about his previous life since he had left; his only thoughts outside of his present reality had been reserved for Marina and Dior. He missed them both a great deal and he longed for them to experience with him the peacefulness of Acerenza.

At Budini's, the Italian morning rite of a cappuccino and a home-baked *cornetto* (croissant) was in full swing. Luca had made certain that the entire town knew that Mark, the young Acerenzese-turned-American-big-shot-against-his-will, had returned to his native roots.

"Even the almighty dollar has not succeeded in keeping our Marco from returning," Luca explained to the townspeople. "The sun, the air, the people, and the childhood memories have been too strong for Marco to resist. How much do people need to be happy? In the end, life must be lived in happiness and self-contentment because it is of such short duration," Luca, the philosopher-king, said. Mark felt that Luca had gauged this very simple, but deeply complex, thought accurately. It was a valuable lesson to keep in mind.

Mark's arrival at Budini's was welcomed with gestures of friendliness and genuine happiness. "Ben tornado, Marco," many of the café customers said. "Welcome back" was the refrain most often repeated by the regular patrons of Budini's. They lined up as if at an Italian wedding reception and heartily shook Mark's hand, or offered a gentle pat on his back. Mark felt as if Marco had indeed returned home.

Hugs and kisses from Amelia Budini shook Mark from his trance. Amelia took Mark's hand and walked him to a stool in front of the counter and then quickly returned to her usual post behind the pastry display. They looked at each other for a long time, until Amelia's eyes welled with tears, betraying her otherwise usual stoicism. Growing up, Amelia had seen Mark every day since he and her brother Gianni were best friends and had been inseparable. Even at five years of age, Amelia had been very fond of Mark because he had always treated her with respect and had never neglected her as her brother had. Amelia had wanted to spend more time playing with Mark and her brother, and would have asked to become a member of the Tre Moschettieri had it not been for her brother's castigations.

"I was heartbroken after you left for America," Amelia confessed, half a century later, "especially since you left without saying good-bye. But no matter. You're back now." The two childhood friends resumed their conversation as if they had never been separated by many intervening decades.

After devouring Amelia's offerings of a *cornetto al cioccolato* (chocolate croissant) and a slice of rice cake (both baked by Amelia just a couple of hours earlier), and drinking the most intensely-flavored cappuccino he had ever tasted, Mark was ready to set out once again to recapture more of the memories he had abandoned so long ago.

"Arrivederci," Mark said as he exited the café.

"A presto," replied Amelia with a smile that lit the room.

CHAPTER 31

D o you remember, Marco, when Father Caius first gave us our chierichetto outfits? All in red with a white rope as a belt and a matching white collar?" Luca asked, referring to the altar boy outfits they'd worn as children. They had entered the cavernous cathedral where they'd spent many hours building up a reservoir of memories that would last a lifetime.

"Si, ricordo benissimo, Luca. I remember well that we were the best chierichetti ever. We never missed a service, and sometimes, we served two masses a day."

Mark remembered vividly the pleasure he had felt as his parents and grandparents sat in the front pews, proud as peacocks, watching every move he made as he assisted Father Caius with Mass.

◆

Marco's family craned their necks so that they could hear every word emanating from Marco as he responded to the priest's prayers, benedictions, and supplications. It was no matter that Mass was celebrated in Latin and Marco did not understand any of it. He knew every word and repeated his chorus from the heart. They may have been words by rote for an eight-year-old, but they were heartfelt because they were the words of God.

In playing out the role of a chierichetto, the timing of the utterances was everything. The priest's reading of the scriptures had to be met with the chierichetto's response exactly on cue. One second too early, and it might interrupt the flow of the reading of the Scriptures by the priest. One second too late, and the response would be cut off either by the priest's subsequent reading or by the general chorus from the parishioners. This was a fully synchronized orchestra with the priest being the conductor, the altar boy being the concert master, and the faithful contributing the background music. Each of the components had an important role to play. All needed to synchronize their respective participations perfectly and harmoniously if the concerto was to be successfully performed.

As he overcame his jitters from his first Mass, the rookie chierichetto gained more and more confidence to the point that Father Caius elevated him to lead chierichetto. Marco would, in time, be the one who held the Scriptures for the priest to read. He would flip pages by memory, without even once looking at the Holy Book. Marco knew every line, every Latin word by memory, every intonation and would flip page after page in perfect timing so that Father Caius would never hesitate, even for a millisecond, at the end of the page.

With the passage of time, Marco's body language was sufficient to alert the other altar boys to fetch and get ready the incense urns, light specific candles, or undertake the various tasks that needed to be done during the service. It was Marco whom Father Caius ultimately chose as the chierichetto who would hold the Holy Chalice as the priest administered communion to the faithful.

◆

Ah, those were wonderful, wondrous days, Mark thought. *Carefree, spiritual days filled with joy and importance.* Mark had felt, even as a youngster, that he had an inside track to God. He believed that every Mass he serviced, every holy word he uttered in church, would bring him closer to God. He often felt as if he was not so much responding to Father Caius's reading of the Scriptures, but rather having a direct conversation with God. His mind and body seemed imbued with a special sanctification that others were not capable of experiencing.

But even at that young age, even in the House of God, it was important to Mark that he be the lead altar boy; that he be Father Caius's chosen one to service the important masses, the ones celebrated on the important religious days, and the ones during the peak times when the cathedral overflowed with the faithful Acerenzesi.

Even at that young age, Mark had a burning ambition to succeed and to lead. His early ambition allowed him to have a special connection with God—closer and more special than his peers, he believed. This type of burning ambition, although at the time purely spiritual in nature, Mark now reasoned, was the seed that would later germinate into the financial and reputational successes he had achieved.

Mark lit a candle, entered a pew, and, in genuflection, remained silent for a very long time. His thoughts wandered off many miles. He questioned whether Father Caius would now be proud of how little Marco had subsequently staked out his life, whether the special connection he once had with God might have been eroded, along life's paths, by his driving ambition, ambition that had grown devoid of any thought of spirituality. Had his youthful and laudable ambition turned into an all-consuming and devouring monster later in life? Had he forgotten how to accommodate his undeniable drive to succeed within the more important element of spirituality?

Luca's gentle grip on Mark's shoulder shook him out of his trance. Luca smiled at his friend. Mark felt that Luca understood that he was searching to find out who he was now and would be in the future; Luca intuited what his friend was thinking.

Luca's words, however, were somewhat more direct. "Marco, we have been here for an hour. Reflection makes the mind healthy and the stomach hungry. We go to Teresa's Trattoria for the best panino al prosciutto di Parma."

And with that irrebuttable statement, the two old friends walked out of the cathedral, a hand on each other's shoulder.

CHAPTER 32

The grape harvest—*la vendemmia*—in Italy in general, and in Acerenza in particular, is a feast for the senses. That period from the middle of October to the end of November is characterized by sunny, mild days and brisk evenings. The harvest moon is all the illumination that's needed to find one's way. On a clear night, millions of fireflies allow for the reading of a book without any artificial props.

It is a wondrous time of year with colors that defy description, sounds that rival the finest rhapsodies, smells that tickle the senses, and tastes that wreak havoc on taste buds. But there is one, and only one, principal player in this seasonal play. While the harvesting of olives has its own special rites, and whereas the picking of fruits such as figs, persimmons, and pomegranates make gourmands squeal with delight, the only legitimate ruler of the harvest season is Bacchus. It is the god of wine who has always dominated this territory in autumn. The white muscatel, red Zinfandel throughout the Italian peninsula, and Aglianico in Acerenza bring an almost fanatical fever into the heart of thousands of communities. Large round white grapes are reserved for dessert *moscato* wines, while purple grapes with a slice of Grana Padano cheese are perfect for snacking. Purebreds, hybrids, natives, immigrants—the grape rules Acerenza with more influence, and more respect, than the Etruscans had engendered many centuries earlier.

Caravans of mules, donkeys, and horse-drawn carts carry these grapes—God's reward for a year of hard work and nurturing—to either communal grottoes for mass production or to personally owned grottoes. Either way, whether with the use of technology or hands and feet, the process is the same: crushing is followed by natural fermentation and the filtering of the *mosto* (grape juice) into large wooden vats where aging occurs.

The entire process of turning grapes into wine hasn't changed much throughout the generations. Every few years, a bit of new technology is introduced, supposedly to make life easier for the winemaker. But these so-called innovations are rarely embraced in full. There is a mysticism to traditional wine making, as there is an individual reputation to maintain. Everybody knows who makes the best wine, who has the best grapes, and who was crowned as last year's *re del vino* (king of wine).

◆

"Marco, take off your shoes and wash your feet with soap and hot water. Roll up your pants to your knees and then come and help me with the crushing," Marco's benevolent grandfather said. Little Marco cherished these days. How important he felt doing a real man's job. It was an important task because the wine wasn't just used for personal sustenance, but was also used as an important currency to barter for other goods and services. Ten liters of red wine could be exchanged for half a year of haircuts from the local *barbiere* or for many loaves of crusty bread from the neighborhood *fornaio*.

And with all this importance that the grape carried, Marco's nonno had entrusted the crushing—the most important step in the process—to him. Little Marco energetically stomped the grapes in one spot, and then in a slow circle, until they were crushed and converted into wine juice. This process went on for hours until his nonno stopped, usually for a bite to eat or for a drink, before resuming the task with renewed vigor.

"Will my feet ever return to normal color?" Marco asked his grandfather, no doubt concerned that, like in Shakespeare's *Macbeth*, all the rubbing in the world would not remove that "damned spot." But some patient rubbing and scrubbing always did the job, although it took several weeks to fully remove all the wine stains. Marco could have cleaned his feet and lower legs more quickly than he did, but he was less than dutiful in scrubbing the stains away because he wanted to show his friends that his grandfather had entrusted him with the important task.

◆

Things had inevitably changed in Acerenza over the years. Caravans of horse-drawn carts were largely replaced by trucks. Paved roads appeared where only dirt paths used to be. And so, progress had slowly crept in to create more efficiency and less backbreaking work. The foot stomping had also been largely, but not completely, replaced by electric crushing machines. But save for these minor variations, the process during la vendemmia largely remained intact.

There seemed to be no need for wholesale changes. For centuries this traditional process had worked well. It would remain thus through many future generations. *What could be more beautiful to witness than the natural conversion of the solid grape into liquid wine?* Mark thought one afternoon. Wine making is an art merged with chemistry, tradition, and subjective personality. It is a process transfused with purity from start to finish. Year after year, it brings joy and satisfaction to the farmer, the vintner, and the consumer and results in substantial annual financial wealth to millions globally. And it all starts with the lonely vintner, the many nonni who, like Mark's nonno, dedicate their lives to a job in which they take pride and which supports their families.

What else can anyone hope for? To what better personal goals and objectives can one aspire? thought Mark as his mind again traveled back to his own corporate accomplishments at home.

CHAPTER 33

When Mark was a child, the Santa Lucia celebration, the Festival of Light, had always been an annual event for which he waited with great anticipation. Santa Lucia was the Saint of Sight and, as such, had always had a special meaning for the Acerenzesi. Santa Lucia and San Canio were considered to be the townspeople's favorite saints, and each were given, at one time or another during the year, a celebration in their honor.

While San Canio, the town's patron saint, was honored with traditional musical processions through the streets of Acerenza, celebrations for Santa Lucia were pure magic. In the days leading up to December 13, the whole town prepared. Every neighborhood—at times consisting of no more than half a dozen intersections—was a participant. The event resulted in an intratown competition that, like the annual Palio in Siena, was intended to honor a common theme, but always resulted in generational competitions that were discussed and debated in all the cafés in town for many days after their completion. Unlike the Tuscan horse race, though, no trophies or county colors of honor were handed out. Nevertheless, the pride in participating during the

Santa Lucia celebration was just as intensely felt. It was neighborhood against neighborhood. The Acerenzesi worked hard, but also played hard. They took no prisoners in either activity.

◆

In the two days leading up to the evening of December 13, Marco and his neighborhood friends went door to door in the Via Sileo neighborhood and collected firewood for the Santa Lucia dedication. He and his colleagues, and many others, toiled for hours, begging for wood and carrying it to the small neighborhood square.

After a couple of days of this hard work, the wood pile was immense. The pyramid-like structure typically grew to a height of up to ten feet, often with a circumference of forty to fifty feet, or more. Dozens of these wooden pyramids grew all over town. Acerenza didn't take a backseat to the great pyramids of Egypt. It may have taken thousands of hardworking slaves to lay the foundations and build the Egyptian structures, but the hard work undertaken by Marco and his friends was, for them, just as laborious and the results just as fulfilling—perhaps even more so.

And so, promptly at twilight on December 13, as the last rays faded beyond the rooftops, dozens of local families in every neighborhood gathered around the wood pyramids. The traditional lighting of the fire was left for the eldest in the neighborhood. Men, women, and children sat on stools or on blankets on the cobblestones, with light and shadow from the growing flames bouncing on their eager and excited faces.

Within minutes, the *minario* (the bonfire) grew and leapt from within itself to the pinnacle of the pyramid, to the delight of the spectators. It was at this time that the food and drink started pouring out of all the neighboring homes. Cheeses, chestnut pies, ricotta-laden cakes, dried fruits, hazelnuts, almonds, and walnuts, and chickpeas and chestnuts for roasting, were washed down with locally made wine, both vintage and sweet white *moscatello*.

Marco and his friends, though, were nowhere to be seen when the food arrived. They were busy running to other bonfires to compare height, circumference, depth, and brightness of flame. Everyone in town knew, year after year, which neighborhoods were in the running for the top spot. There would never be a crowning of the winner, though. Debates would begin the very next morning at Budini's and all the other cafés in town, and would last for days until fatigue brought in a consensual winner, but always, and necessarily, with vocal dissenting votes.

And in this way, the celebrations all over town, separate but unified in a common purpose, went late into the night, until the fire had turned into a pile of ashes.

Marco was awed by the Santa Lucia minario. The bonfire was magical, the sweets and food he ate were a rare treat, and the competition among neighborhoods was fierce but exhilarating. When it was finally time to retire for the night, he would lay awake for hours playing and replaying the entire evening. What could they do next year to make their minario bigger and better? And how could he, Marco, better contribute to ensure that "his" bonfire would be declared the winner? The drive to succeed occupied little Marco at a young age.

◆

Standing in the square for Acerenza's celebration on December 13, Mark was glad to see that the Santa Lucia tradition had survived the many years. The bonfires were not, admittedly as plentiful around town as he remembered them as a child, but the festivities were just as much fun and intensely felt, and the food and drink were exactly as he remembered them.

Mark smiled broadly as Luca handed him roasted chestnuts and a glass of sweet moscatello. While, technically speaking, Luca was from a different neighborhood, nevertheless, he was a "guest" of the Via Sileo clan on this night.

"Come on, Luca," said Mark. "Let's go see what kind of minario our colleagues in the other neighborhoods have concocted." And thus, the two friends disappeared in the dark night searching for memories of yesteryear, while reliving those memories half a century later.

At home that night, after the celebrations had ended, Mark wondered when he had last participated in such simple a pleasure as gathering with neighbors in a common festivity to which everyone was invited and at which everyone attended. No RSVPs were needed. No discussion of dress code was relevant. All one needed to do was show up, contribute food or drink as best they could, and, thereupon, engage in a celebration of life—using Santa Lucia as the excuse.

As Mark's thoughts wandered back to his last few days at Santius, he felt a personal satisfaction that he had not experienced for many years. It was incredible, he thought, that an event as basic as what he had just experienced, could so immeasurably help fill the inexplicable inner vacuum that had developed during his previous corporate existence.

CHAPTER 34

Mark had been in Acerenza for four weeks. While he had spoken with his wife, Marina, every day and with his daughter, Dior, several times a week, nevertheless, Mark missed them both terribly. True, he had been busy catching up and reconnecting with the people and places that had formed an important foundation for the person he turned out to be, but he longed for discussions with his wife, the plans they regularly made for social activities, their frequent visits to their favorite cafés for a lazy cappuccino and biscotti, and their idle time during the weekend. And he also missed his energetic talks with Dior, who would unfailingly provide an update on her latest adventure or misadventure. Mark usually came out of those father-daughter discussions reenergized. Often, Dior's views provoked him into deep thought and, at times, a rethinking of ideas that he had believed had safely been determined.

During a recent phone conversation, Marina expressed concern about Mark's voluntary refuge into his past.

"I understand your need to be alone for a while to sort out your conflicting internal values," Marina said, "but I want to be part of your considerations and be near you while you figure everything out."

It was a quick family decision that Marina and Dior would join Mark in Acerenza to spend an old-fashioned small town Christmas together. Marina and Dior were looking forward to traveling to Italy and Mark was excited to show his family the festive sights and sounds of his hometown.

Marina and Dior arrived in Acerenza one week before Christmas, but the holiday season was well under way. In fact, the end of the Santa Lucia festivities coincided with the serious start of the Christmas celebrations—much like Macy's Thanksgiving Day parade in New York paved the way for the start of Christmas preparations in the United States.

After their first family dinner in Acerenza, Mark and Marina dressed up in their Sunday finest and walked to the main piazza for the nightly ritual played out in every city, town, and village on the entire peninsula: *la passeggiata* (the nightly stroll). La passeggiata has been an Italian tradition since time immemorial, but it is not simply a lengthy walk to work off the hefty dinner just consumed. No, it is the highlight of the day. It is a time when Italians dress up and parade their feathers, much like peacocks, to be admired by others. Life unfolds naturally during la passeggiata. Every couple is bodily entwined in some form: teenagers and other unmarried couples drape their arms and hands over their loved ones so tightly that there is the risk of blood clotting; newlyweds walk hand-in-hand, staring into each another's eyes as if searching for secrets; middle-aged couples devote their energy and attention more to their offspring in tow than to one another; and the elder statesmen, arm-in-arm and formal in appearance, take in the show all around them and often glide slowly with an air of confidence and elegance that only age and maturity can bring. The parade is endless. Couples walk from one end of the square to the other, and then back again and again and again. And so it goes, every night, weather permitting.

It is a noble tradition that allows families, neighbors, and townspeople to come together to stop and chat for a minute or to tip one's hat or shake the hand of an acquaintance. Often, friends congregate after la passeggiata at a favorite bar or café for an after-dinner drink.

In Acerenza, the drink de rigueur is the Amaro Lucano—a bitter alcoholic drink made in Acerenza's own province of Basilicata. Basilicata was once known as Lucania; hence, the name Amaro Lucano, or literally, "bitter Lucano."

"What a civilized way to the end the day," Marina said, as they strolled through the piazza. "It's certainly different than plunking down on the couch with a beer in hand to watch a rerun of *Survivor*."

While a somewhat exaggerated comparison, Mark recognized that Marina was struck by the vastly more familial lifestyle in Italy compared to what they were both used to back home.

That night, Marina and Mark fell asleep with the curtains open to allow the smiling stars a peek at their embrace that lasted until dawn.

"So Dad, tell me about your stay here. How you have been spending your days and what decisions you have made?" Dior asked the next morning at breakfast. Mark looked into Dior's limpid blue eyes; they were like her mother's. They evidenced an unmistakable sincerity of character, a gentleness of spirit, and a childish curiosity that merged into traits of generosity, kindness, and playfulness. They were the traits of Marina that Mark had loved for almost four decades, and they were the same traits Dior would carry with her in life. Dior had also inherited many things from Mark, including ambition, incisiveness, analytical logic, integrity, and a spiritual and romantic soul. All in all, Dior was a complex young woman who had been Mark's pride and joy from her birth.

Dior's perplexed stare brought Mark to real time. "Dior, my stay here has opened my eyes to a different way of life. Meeting these people and participating in their daily activities has reawakened in me the need to slow down my life and emphasize the ideals that we tend to lose as we go about our days. I am learning that we always must live life in a way that satisfies our moral principles. These are essential traits that are subjective to the individual and cannot normally be categorized as right or wrong. These personal principles are not governed by laws or regulations. They are governed by rules that are, in fact, higher and more noble than prescribed laws. They are directed by one's own view of how he wants to be known by his family, friends, and peers during his life, and how he wishes to be remembered after his passing."

Dior contemplated her father's comments. Her eyes seemed to shine more than usual as she considered the progress of her own young life. She wanted to dig further.

"Dad, you told Mom and me about your confrontation with Mr. Cavendish and how it led to your resignation from Santius. I understand that part, and can see how this would cause you to rethink your personal career path going forward, but I don't quite understand how that incident has forced you into a total reevaluation of your whole life. From where I am sitting, you have a wonderful life, with a family that worships you and a community that respects you. What am I missing?"

For a moment, Mark was back at Santius, reliving his unsavory saga with Cavendish. Mark again wondered whether the entire episode may have simply been a normal disagreement in the course of business. *Did I later exaggerate the encounter to justify my departure?* Mark thought. *Was I a poor loser?* Perhaps Mark's resignation was not due to the seeming erosion of his integrity, but was because he had wanted a dramatic change in his life. Perhaps his values had changed and Santius had been the catalyst to effect that change. Perhaps Mark had been too harsh on himself.

As these thoughts continued to swirl around his head, Mark responded to Dior's comments. "It was more than a difference of opinion, Dior. I believed then, and believe now, that the viability of Santius lay in the strategy that I recommended. The status quo for Santius will eventually lead to its destruction because it will cause the company to lose its relevance as a separate entity. Once the board, for short-term and selfish personal gain, took a different position, I had no choice but to resign—"

Dior interrupted, "But you did resign, Dad. You resigned from Santius precisely because you disagreed with the board."

"Well, I didn't resign because of the disagreement over the corporate strategy. In fact, I did the opposite. I not only stayed on, but told the Santius shareholders that I was prepared to accept the board's decision and stay as CEO to implement it. This was wrong. I shouldn't have compromised my views. Maybe there were other reasons that led to my inner conflict. Maybe I subconsciously knew I needed to change. What I'm saying is that perhaps I used the situation at Santius to make changes in my own life."

In questioning her father, Dior seemed to be searching for a lesson to adopt for her own fledgling career. It almost seemed as if she wanted to know the secret to leading a successful and happy life. This was not idle chatter on her part or an exchange of gossip with her father. She wanted to ensure that her own professional career would be led in a way that neither she nor others could later question.

"Even if you did compromise your own personal views by what you said in your speech to the shareholders, what harm did you do? You later did the right thing and resigned, didn't you? What's the problem?"

It was a relief for Mark to deal with the legal repercussions of his actions. Legal issues, for him, had always been much easier to resolve than matters dealing with integrity-compromising executive decisions.

"The problem is that my speech misled many Santius investors into believing that I was not worried and that all was well with the company. That conclusion was based on my words—words which were consciously uttered to create a false conclusion. Those words could create potential legal damages if any of Santius's investors acted on them. But, what worries me the most, it that my speech could result in the very thing that drove Cavendish and the board to stake their position: short-term personal gain. In other words, greed."

Dior reflected on these comments in silence. She then smiled sympathetically at her dad and said, "Dad, I believe you're going through a midlife crisis. God, I'm not looking forward to that stage in my life."

"Let me get Mom so that you can show us around town. I want to work up an appetite for lunch. I'm dying for a bowl of pasta."

Perhaps Dante Alighieri had also been going through a midlife crisis as he embarked on his journey in the Divine Comedy, Mark thought to himself.

CHAPTER 35

Christmas Eve in Acerenza was a time for families to stay together, pray together, and rejoice in the imminent birth of Baby Jesus. The Gentile clan spent that special evening at Luca Moranni's house, where Luca's wife, Anna, and their two teenage daughters, who had come home for the holidays, had been preparing the Christmas Eve meal for two days.

Tradition was everything. This was not a time for the *nuova cucina* or innovative dishes. Anna had learned from her mother, who, in turn, had learned from hers, as it had been for generations.

The smells permeating the Morannis' house were intoxicating. Indeed, that evening, as the Gentile family walked over to Luca's home, the smells throughout the streets were indescribably appetizing. From virtually every open window or door, the Gentiles inhaled the delicious smell of freshly roasted chestnuts, pies, and pastries filled with ricotta and sprinkled with cinnamon powder and grated chocolate. Even the most particular and creative chef would have marveled at the aroma of the tomato sauces—those deceptively simple smells of orchard-grown tomatoes bottled in the fall with basil, oregano, salt, and garlic cooking on an open flame.

Prominently, by the window, Mark noticed the Morannis' beautiful Christmas tree. Mark did not remember Christmas trees back in his childhood in Acerenza. But, as he reminded himself, that recollection was half a century old. Now, the world had shrunk. Borders had been lifted. Proprietary traditions had been unblocked and were shared worldwide. The Internet, HD television, and satellite-driven communication had also arrived here and it seemed that Acerenza had appropriated the beautiful tradition of Christmas trees, lit by multicolored bulbs, with ornaments of all types, shapes, and sizes hanging from the branches. Even the traditional exchange of Christmas gifts, either after midnight on Christmas Eve or early on Christmas morning, had reached Acerenza. Nevertheless, because of the generosity of La Befana, Epiphany had always been, and to some extent, continued to be, the portent of gifts for children.

La Befana was a benevolent witch who rode a broom looking for the Christ Child's manger in Bethlehem each year. Legend had it that the Three Wise Men had stopped at La Befana's hut to ask for directions to Bethlehem and had invited her to join them in their travels. La Befana refused. Later, she saw a light in the skies and realized her mission was to travel to Bethlehem. La Befana gathered some toys that had belonged to her own deceased child, and set out to find the Three Wise Men and the stable. But despite her best efforts, she never found the manger. Now, each year, she traveled on her broom and left gifts for the good children all over Italy, Acerenzesi included, and pieces of charcoal for the undeserving ones.

◆

Marco hung the long hand-knitted sock, made by his mother specifically for the occasion, on the mantelpiece on the eve of Epiphany. Early the next morning, he woke up to see whether La Befana had adjudged his behavior during the past year to have been acceptable and thereby worthy of candy, chocolates, and sweet dried fruits, or if she considered his behavior less than exemplary, and thereby condemned him to receive a sock full of ashes and coal.

With excited anticipation, little Marco hesitantly drove his hand down into the sock, and as his little fingers touched and felt its contents, a broad smile formed on his lips and relief filled his eyes. Once again, he had received a passing grade from La Befana. Once again, little Marco had succeeded in keeping secret his occasional grand theft of fruits and other edibles from the nearby orchards with the other two moschettieri.

◆

The Moranni meal on Christmas Eve was a spectacularly colorful, and yet simple, affair. The large wooden table had almost certainly been in the family for dozens of years. It showed gouges and cuts aplenty and was at least six inches of solid natural wood. The place settings consisted of beautiful hand-painted clay plates, crafted by Luca and his family. No two plates were the same size or shape, and yet their symmetry was stunning. They were made for that antique and asymmetrical table. Next to each plate was a cloth napkin, hand-stitched by Anna, and embroidered with a Christmas theme. At the center of the table was a large wooden tray with a variety of shelled hazelnuts, walnuts, and almonds, as well as dried figs, apricots, and dates. The fruits and nuts were mainly to munch on in between courses, but they also decorated the table in celebration of the upcoming Holy Birth. Vintage local red Aglianico wine was in small wooden flasks, dispersed around the table, just as Mark remembered at his nonno's house.

In the old days, twenty-four hours before Christmas, the Acerenzesi observed strict fasting. However, with the passage of time, the fasting had largely been abandoned in favor of a less restrictive "no meat" meal. The *cenone* (feast) began with a stracciatella soup, a form of egg-drop soup with *stelline* (miniature star-shaped pasta), followed by a toast to everyone's health, happiness, and prosperity—in that order. Then the *ortaggi*, cut-up vegetables lightly grilled and simply sprinkled with sea salt and extra-virgin olive oil, was served, followed by another toast to the health of each other's families, the members of which were named one by one. This was followed by homemade spaghetti, hand-drawn by Anna that very afternoon, with a simple tomato, basil, and anchovy sauce. The spaghetti dish was heavenly in taste, precisely because of its simplicity and freshness. Its indescribable aroma permeated the kitchen and the dining room, and spilled out into the street through the partially opened window. Cod filets marinated and grilled on a wire rack placed on live coals in Anna's kitchen followed. By now, Luca was struggling to come up with additional references for toasts, but he unfailingly managed to do so over and over and over again.

Luca announced a break in the meal, as he proudly loosened his belt. "It's time," he said, "to gather around the open hearth and sing Italian Christmas carols." Everyone belted out the arias with fervor, and had good fun, although admittedly, the words flowed more easily from Luca, Anna, and their two children than from Mark. Marina and Dior, armed with only a conversational knowledge of Italian, hummed along and heartily sang the chorus lines. The festive atmosphere was enhanced when Luca turned off of all the lights in the living room. The leaping flames of the fire were the only source of light in the room.

Then, it was time for dessert—*il dolce*. Anna brought out tray after tray laden with slices of cheesecake; little *scarpelle* with *vino cotto* (fried doughnut-like dumplings dunked in sweet wine juice); triangular, square, and circular clusters of almonds toasted in toffee; and finally, a *granita di caffè*, crushed ice drowned in sweetened espresso, with a drop or two of liqueur.

As the coffee was served, Marina asked, while smiling, whether the espresso was decaffeinated. The Morannis took Marina's question as a joke and laughed heartily. "Hai sentito, Anna? Ha chiesto se il caffè fosse decaffeinato" (Did you hear, Anna? She asked if the coffee is decaffeinated), Luca struggled to say in between howls of laughter. Mark didn't have the heart to sober up Luca by confiding that Marina had been quite serious in asking for decaf espresso. She only drank decaf coffee at home. That evening, though, Marina made an exception to her self-imposed rule. She later admitted that the espresso granita was the most delicious coffee dessert she had ever tasted. Not a word was said about the liquor that had been stealthily added by Luca.

Luca proposed one final toast. "Che Dio ci porti fortuna a tutti, e pace in tutto il mondo" (may God bring good fortune to us here and may He also bring peace to the world). The dessert wine for this last toast was a sweet white moscatello wine. Its aromas reminded Mark of the local vineyards that he had once known so well. Childhood memories came rushing back.

As a final act that Christmas Eve, the Moranni and Gentile families walked together in the brisk evening air to the cathedral to view the life-size *presepio* (nativity scene), and witness the birth of the Redeemer.

Later, back at home, Marina, Dior, and Mark excitedly talked about the evening they had just spent with their friends. "I now understand, like never before, what it means to spend a special day with family and friends," Dior said.

"The friendliness and generosity of the Morannis made this a wonderful Christmas Eve," Marina said, "and the simplicity of their customs and the genuineness of their hospitality was truly touching."

"It's hard to explain," Dior said, "but I've never felt closer to the spirituality of Christmas than I did this evening." No one was in any hurry to go to bed. The Gentile family had their individually felt emotions to share with one another.

Finally, Dior ended the marathon day. "Time for bed. Dad, after this evening, I understand why you came here to unwind and regroup. This is as close to heaven as I've experienced. See you both in the morning." Dior kissed her parents good night before walking up the stairs to her room.

Marina hugged Mark and sleepily said, "I second that," and walked up the stairs to their bedroom. It seemed that the caffeine in her espresso had been dissolved by the added liqueur; Marina fell into a deep sleep almost the moment her head hit the pillow.

Mark, on the other hand, stood by the window for a long time, staring out at the dark and lonely street below. He pondered what he had become. He thought about his past struggles which led him to his current station in life. He played out in his mind the importance of his family, which he adored. For the first time since he had arrived in

Acerenza, he felt fully at peace with himself. He felt a satisfaction with who he was. He felt confident about the future, and his role in it.

Cavendish now seemed not only distant, but, indeed, a figment of his imagination, a stranger in his current environment. His experiences at Santius felt like they had happened a lifetime ago and in a different world.

Optimism flowed through his veins. Yes, Mark's best days were ahead of him. Whatever reason had prompted his departure, he now knew he had made the right decision to leave. He knew that he had also made the correct choice in picking Acerenza as the environment in which either to redeem himself or simply to reenergize and begin on a different path.

Mark joined Marina in bed, though he knew it was unlikely he would sleep much that night.

CHAPTER 36

On Christmas morning, Acerenza was beautiful and pristine. The sun's rays shone brightly on a fresh blanket of snow. The town had become a beautiful bride in white. Tufts of smoke emanated from the rooftop chimneys and hung crystallized in the cold air, as if they were reluctant to leave such a beautiful sight.

By midmorning, Via Sileo was active. Children donned their finest coats, hats, and gloves, and excitedly threw snowballs at all moving targets. Their parents told them to hurry their steps so that they would not be late for Mass.

The Gentile family had no desire for breakfast. The feast from the night before was enough to nourish them for days. A simple homemade espresso was the perfect start to the day. Cups in hand, Mark, Dior, and Marina stood by the second floor window and stared silently at the white mountains piercing a sunny, azure sky. "There are no problems in the world…" whispered Marina, pointing toward the landscape.

"Certainly no problems that can't be solved," Mark said with a smile.

"Buon Natale!" exclaimed Luca, Anna, and their daughters as they let themselves into the house.

"Pieno di gioia e di buona salute" (full of happiness and health), Anna added, with kisses and embraces all around.

Luca's visit reminded Mark of the ancient tradition in Acerenza of leaving front doors open—even in the cold days of December and January—to allow the free entry of neighbors, friends, and relatives. The community visited one another during holiday celebrations and exchanged their good wishes for happiness, good health, and prosperity. Usually, there was a pecking order. The eldest, the town patriarchs, would be visited upon by the younger generations, as a sign of respect for their seniority and, therefore, their assumed wisdom. The Gentile family, being visitors, were thrust in the role of elders on this occasion and, as a result, a continuing parade of well-wishers ensued, entering into, and egressing from, the Gentile household. In the house, on the steps, and on the street, they seized the opportunity to exchange Christmas greetings among themselves.

When the crowds dwindled, Dior expressed her surprise. "This is amazing. You didn't even know the majority of these people, and yet they all came just to give us their Christmas wishes." Mark was happy to see that his daughter realized that true reward lies in conducting oneself in a way that expresses a sentiment of altruism, of doing something not because of expected reciprocity, but because it causes joy in the recipient.

CHAPTER 37

Mark remembered the road to his family's vineyard, Alvanello, as steep and arduous. Their mule, Mark recalled, had a difficult time climbing with the heavy chests of fruits, vegetables, and grapes on its back. As Mark's grandfather aged, he used to walk slowly behind the mule, holding on to its tail as it climbed the hill. The mule labored mightily carrying the heavy load and dragging along Mark's grandfather at the same time.

But the municipality had since built a paved road that wound down the mountain. Automobiles replaced the tails of mules, and trucks replaced the mules altogether.

That Christmas afternoon, as Mark drove his family down to Alvanello in the valley, Marina asked him to stop the car for a moment, searched in her oversized bag, and drew out a sketchpad. She got out of the car and raised her coat collar to protect herself from the December chills. Marina found a large rock beside the road, brushed away the snow, and sat down to sketch the mountainside, from the frozen River Bradano down below, all the way up to the town of Pietragalla which sat on a neighboring mountain.

Marina is a Renaissance woman, Mark thought with affection, as he watched his wife from the car. She was equally at ease reading Petrarch and Stendhal or sketching and painting, as she was solving a difficult math problem or uncovering a scientific issue. Mark had loved her dearly for almost forty years, but never more than during those twenty minutes when she was transfixed by the beauty around her, struggling to capture a tiny segment of that beauty on her sketchpad.

"Impossible!" exclaimed an exasperated Marina, as she hurried back to the warmth of the car. "Absolutely impossible to capture even a fraction of what I see here, what I am experiencing..." her voice trailed off. Indeed, even if an artist could paint the purity of the freshly fallen snow, the trees half-naked and seemingly shivering in the cold, the beauty of mountain ranges as far as the eye could see, and the light columns of smoke from the chimneys of farm houses, how could he, even Cézanne or Renoir, ever capture the delicious silence of isolation? How does an artist paint their tingling emotions as they are awed by the overwhelming peace and tranquility of nature?

Impossible indeed, thought Mark. He remembered *Il Deserto dei Tartari*, an Italian novel he had read many years earlier when he used to find the time to read a good book. Unlike the expectancy and fear of isolation that appeared in that novel, the tranquil isolation he found here was calming; it enveloped him and put his soul at ease. The beauty of the place created an optimism that could repair any problem, no matter how insoluble it seemed—in theory.

Once at the ungated entrance to Alvanello, Mark parked the car and the three solitary figures marched toward the farmhouse where Mark had many years earlier locked in so many memories. There was the neighbor's famous cherry tree where Mark's grandfather had committed grand larceny many years earlier, the *corpus delicti*, as it were. And there were the white and black fig trees that still produced the juiciest figs Mark had ever tasted. Mark also spotted the stream that carried the purest and coldest water, from an underground mountain spring, he had ever tasted.

"We used to drink this water by cupping a vine leaf," Mark told Marina. "Nature provided us with almost everything we needed for our daily existence. We ate and drank nature's purity long before nutritionists revoked processed foods in favor of everything organic."

It was getting chilly and the soft clattering of everyone's teeth told Marina it was time to head back. She tried to nudge her husband back toward the car, but Mark had other ideas. He led Marina and Dior to the farmhouse. Mark pulled out a key from underneath a nearby rock and opened the front door. The farmhouse had been well maintained by Marcello during the vine-growing season, but from the end of November through March, the house remained vacant. It was dark inside, but Mark's vivid memories seemed to light up the room. By rote, Mark piled some logs into the fireplace and lit them with the five-inch-long matches specially made to light stubborn fires. Soon, the crackling flames brought light and warmth to the room—a room much smaller than Mark remembered.

Mark, Marina, and Dior sat on wooden stools around the fire, rubbing their hands in the warmth. Mark could see his grandfather's kind face in the dancing flames. He could also see himself as little Marco, ready to listen to another mesmerizing tale from his nonno. His grandfather never disappointed.

Marina touched Mark's hand and brought him back to real time. While reluctant to interrupt her husband's recollections of his youth, Marina knew it was time to go. "It's getting dark and we should be heading back." She put her head on his shoulder and softly whispered, "Enough memories for one day."

This Christmas at Acerenza would go down as the most memorable Christmas ever experienced by the Gentile family.

CHAPTER 38

The Christmas festivities continued the entire week, right through January 6, the Feast of the Epiphany.

Every day during this festive period, the cathedral was crowded. The faithful attended church not just to celebrate Mass, but also to witness the presepio. The presepio in Acerenza's main square in front of the cathedral had become legendary. Statues of the Virgin Mary, baby Jesus, Joseph, and the Three Wise Men bearing gifts were life-like. They looked especially real because the Acerenzesi built a perfect replica of the stable equipped with two live miniature donkeys. Elder Acerenzesi took turns standing guard at the entrance to the stable, wearing shepherd hats and playing Christmas tunes on their pipes.

Mark fondly remembered dozens of vendors lining the main street during his childhood with carts full of dried fruits, chocolates, candies, and toys. He would spend hours with his friends exploring these delights and he would endlessly strategize tactics to persuade his benign grandfather to buy him a chocolate bar or candies "imported" from faraway Rome. Mark was grateful that even with the passage of decades, not much had changed in Acerenza at this wonderful time of year. The presepio was still an awesome sight, especially at night, with the moon being the only illumination to guide the Wise Men to their destination and to keep the shepherds company. In the main street, vendors still offered the young Acerenzesi imported delights, not only from faraway Rome, but now also from the four corners of the globe.

Since Acerenza's industry was, essentially, farming, there were no factories to shut down, no service industry to interrupt, and no man-ufacturing equipment to keep running. Indeed, after la vendemmia was over, there was little work for the Acerenzesi to do that couldn't be done on their own schedule. Nature was taking a rest until late February when everything would be readied for the plowing, plant-ing, and feedings for the upcoming season. True, there was fruit to dry, jams and sauces to make, vegetables to pickle, sausages and prosciutto to salt and age, and animals to feed and clean, but these were tasks that would be accomplished on the Acerenzesi's own time. Mother Nature had her own schedule and the Acerenzesi had long ago structured their lives into seasonal tasks rather than mandatory daily activities.

While Christmas and New Year's were the culminating celebra-tions of the season, Santa Lucia actually marked the beginning of the festivities that would continue up to and including Epiphany. From then onward, for the next seven weeks, Acerenza went into a peaceful slumber. Work activities were kept to a minimum, and socially reconnecting with family, friends, and neighbors was the principal occupation.

It was during this period that the latest political scandals were debated, the passion of soccer elevated to new heights, and the expec-tations for the new season of farming were discussed. Cafés were fully patronized during this time. Barber shops, which doubled as gossip centers, were also running at full capacity.

Indeed, this period of manual and physical inactivity was, in fact, a busy time. It was as if this spiritual reconnection among the townspeople was their annual reward for a job well done during the previous year. It was their "bonus," not counted in dollars, but in something much more important and much more fulfilling: the ability to reenergize physically, socially, and spiritually. It was a time when the important activities centered on catching up with God, friends, and one's own internal spiritual needs.

It was a perfect time for Mark to be in Acerenza. The entire citizenry seemed to be on a personal odyssey to reestablish a connection with themselves, their families, and their friends as well.

CHAPTER 39

The day after New Year's, Dior readied herself for her journey back home. She had an important project that her employer, Merkson, had entrusted to her, and her eyes twinkled in anticipation of getting started as soon as she returned.

"Dad, it's time for you to get back in the saddle, no? You've been here almost nine weeks. Haven't you sorted everything out already?" she asked, even though she knew her father's response.

"Almost, sweetheart. Every day, I get closer and closer to knowing what my soul needs, but I need to stay a bit longer. Besides, Luca and Anna have invited your mom and me to help out with cheese making and the curing and salting of meats. When that's done, we'll see, but that may take awhile." Mark winked at Dior and smiled at the prospect of an extended stay in Italy.

Dior embraced her father lovingly and simply said, "I love you, Dad. Take care of yourself and Mom. I'll miss you, and I look forward to your return."

Mark and Marina helped Dior to the piazza for her bus trip to the station and the start of her long journey back home. After final good-byes, Mark and his wife headed into Budini's for a steaming morning cappuccino and cornetto—what had, for them, become a favorite routine and a delicious start to their day.

CHAPTER 40

It was Gaetano's Barber Shop where Mark went for his monthly haircut. While the owners had changed several times since his childhood, Mark had been delighted to see that the new owner, Gaetano's grandson (also named Gaetano according to the Italian custom of naming the eldest grandson after his grandfather), had retained many of the shop's old customs. The new world of Gillette and Schick, to be sure, had long since arrived in Acerenza. Men, by and large, now shaved themselves in the morning with disposable razors. But now and again, they felt the need to be served and pampered at Gaetano's "spa." Particularly during the inter-seasonal slumber, Acerenza's men became willing inmates of the Gaetano spa for several hours, receiving a shampoo, haircut, and shave with a traditional straight razor, a dying art which transcended generations.

And when the pampering was completed, the satisfied customers would simply move from the barber's chair to a waiting chair against the wall, ready to idle way the hours with gossip and small talk. These episodes were an intricate part of the fabric of life in this part of the world. It was a time for regenerating the soul and reenergizing the body, for soon the hard labors would again begin and there would be little time for idleness. Messrs. Gillette and Schick would be happy when early March rolled around so that their profit margins—as modest as they may have been from the Acerenzesi—would once again, at least until Santa Lucia, be reactivated.

During this seasonal interlude, as Mark sat in the chair with Gaetano fussing over him, his mind went back many decades earlier to when his mother, Maria, insisted that he learn a trade so that he would not need to toil on the farms as she and his father had. At five years of age, little Marco began his apprenticeship at the barber shop, watching intensely the barber's every move, fascinated, and, at the same time, fearful, at the thought that someday soon, he too would need to service the clientele at Gaetano's. For Marco, the straight razor became his personal threshold of fear to overcome.

That day, Gaetano treated Mark like royalty with a shampoo, hair styling, neck and head massage, herbal hair treatment, straight-razor shave, and facial. As Mark began his second hour of "spa treatment," vivid memories of his apprenticeship flooded back.

◆

While apprenticing at Gaetano's, little Marco was routinely sent to the bakery next door to fetch live coals in a large aluminum pail. He proudly spread the coals in a flat, open container in the barber shop, and thereupon peeled an orange, cut the peels in small pieces, and threw them randomly on the hot coals in order to abate the smoke and the carbon dioxide from the charcoal. In those days, the hot coals were the only source of heat to cut into the February chills. Marco repeated this process several times a day, each time when the coals lost their glow and turned into ash. Marco's simple reward for this task was a couple of orange slices each time, the leftovers from the peeled oranges. The rest of the orange slices were put on a plate and offered to the customers in the barber shop.

These were, indeed, heady days for little Marco. He was proud to be the designee for such an important job, and he was especially proud to receive his reward for a job well done. His family's departure for Canada became Marco's only barrier to becoming Acerenza's best, and probably most ambitious, hair stylist.

◆

At a very young age, it seemed, Mark had learned an important lesson that had become his *modus operandi* later in his business life: set a goal, accomplish it well, and you will be appropriately rewarded for it.

CHAPTER 41

Except for calls from Marina and Dior before their arrival in Acerenza, Mark's cell phone had remained silent. He had not told any of his former colleagues that he was leaving town for a lengthy period of time. Only his family and closest circle of friends were aware of his whereabouts. He had felt it important to dislodge himself totally from his regular surroundings and from his habitual circle of contacts, at least temporarily.

So it was with some surprise, then, that his phone rang late one day with the customary long-distance tone. "Pronto," Mark answered instinctively in Italian.

"Mark, is that you?" inquired a distant voice. "You've already forgotten how to say hello?" teased John Markham.

Mark and John had been friends for over two decades. John had once been a high-powered executive at Energy Plus, a corporation that managed a number of nuclear reactors for several large electric companies. John had been a wandering soul and he had concluded many years earlier that he wanted off the executive treadmill. He started his own executive search firm which specialized in recruiting executives for technical positions in the energy and automobile industries. It was in this capacity that Mark had met him.

John had recruited several key executives for Santius over the years. All had been highly successful hires. John had an uncanny ability to match the right person for the appropriate role. He would do so by conducting lengthy and repeated investigations of the backgrounds of the candidates he presented. Mark couldn't remember a single instance when John's recommendations had not been accepted, and not one time when John had been wrong or incomplete in his assessments. As a result, a trusting professional relationship had been established between the two, as well as a personal friendship that had lasted many years. John was one of the few individuals who had been given Mark's private phone number, and one of the only people to know Mark's whereabouts and the reason for his voluntary "sabbatical."

"How's Marina, Mark? I phoned Dior the other day and she told me that you had become a willing victim of the mesmerizing beauty of your native town and that it would be difficult to slide you back into your old routine." Indeed, Mark had had the thought that per-haps it was time to dramatically change his lifestyle and his life. He had been considering starting a small business in Acerenza that would keep him busy and, at the same time, provide a life that would be more serene and less stressful.

"No, there was never any serious thought that I would abandon everything I've worked for in over three decades—as tempting as that may be—in favor of pastoral simplicity," Mark lied.

In reality, however, Mark had been considering leaving his life in Canada behind and becoming a full-time vintner at his family's vine-yards at Alvanello. The more Mark thought about the possibility of an Acerenzese wine business, the more it became realistic to achieve, and the more quickly the adrenaline flowed through his veins. Rather than selling his grapes wholesale to the town cooperative, he had reasoned, he could manufacture his own wine, create his own label, and market his product in Europe and elsewhere in the world. He had considered the pros and cons of starting his own brand with the attendant higher risks, but potentially much higher financial rewards, versus private labeling for established brands. Mark had advanced the idea in his own mind to the point of creating revenue and expense pro forma statements, and had developed a draft profit and loss statement at one-, three-, and five-year intervals.

Of course, these were all financial issues with which Mark had deep familiarity, since these important exercises were preconditions to all the private and public offerings that he had overseen at Santius. Mark had spent countless hours and innumerable days and weeks reviewing similar financial issues with Santius's financial experts, external lawyers, and accountants in the preparation of numerous offering memoranda or prospectuses.

Mark had discussed the possibility of assuming full-time responsibility over the winemaking business with Marina. They both decided that he could not pursue the project alone and full time. The principal reason was quite simple: as much as Mark had come to love Acerenza, its beauty, its people, and its peace, he needed more activity than what the village offered. Acerenza was an idyllic paradise full of cherished memories of his past, which had shaped his very being. Mark's recent return to this environment had reaffirmed the tremendous sacrifices his parents made in leaving behind the environment in which they were born and going to a foreign land, full of uncertainties and risks, to provide an opportunity for their son to lead a better life. Ironically, however, so successful had Mark been in fulfilling his parents', and his own, ambitions, that he felt there could now be no turning back to the life his parents had left behind.

Indeed, Mark had decided that his life would continue in "America," but with a more, as yet undefined, spiritual balance, and with a new set of priorities.

"I am in the process of restructuring my vineyards, John. These have been in the care of a trusted employee for many years and I have traditionally had little involvement in their operations, as modest as they have been. But I am now taking over the wine production. Whatever direction this takes, however, I know that I do not want to be a resident vintner for this venture."

Mark thought for a moment. "I'm putting together an infrastructure of experienced and knowledgeable winemakers to run the operations. I've recently spoken with a financial controller who will oversee the finance side of the business, and I've met with a marketing team that will search out wine markets. I'm personally evaluating the financial viability of this venture and I'll obtain financing for equipment, marketing, and plant capital expenditures. We should be ready to go starting with next year's harvest."

John received this news from his friend in stunned silence. It was clear that Mark had considered this business venture carefully and in detail. John knew his friend well enough to realize that any attempt to discourage or dissuade him would be futile, at least at that moment.

"This sounds exciting, Mark. But if your intention is to return home, how will you supervise your investment from a distance?"

Mark was quick to reply. "The key to the success of any business is having a clear vision of the mission and a superb team that believes in that vision and knows how to implement it. I have created the vision and am attempting to finalize the team that will see it through. With the aid of technology and open communication, we could succeed. After all, John, that's how global companies operate. The concept is created in the company's headquarters and is then rolled out in dozens of countries. My task is infinitely easier. The concept is simple and its venue is in one location only, Acerenza. Besides, it would be a huge bonus to personally come to Acerenza three or four weeks every autumn to enjoy seeing the fruits of our labor…and to reconnect with my roots."

John had intended to have a serious discussion with Mark about his friend's career path. However, John felt this was not the appropriate time. "Mark, how would you like to show your old friend the sights and sounds of your hometown? Dior spoke so excitedly of her experiences there at Christmas, that she got me thinking that this is something I want to see for myself. If you agree, I can be there in a week. What do you say, old buddy?"

And so, the two friends agreed that John would arrive in Italy a week later, and that Mark would pick him up at the airport in Rome.

Mark was excited at the thought of John's visit. It would be good to reconnect with the world he had temporarily left behind. Besides, he was interested to hear what proposal John had in mind to discuss with him. He knew that the main reason for his friend's call and his intended visit was not so much to enjoy the scenery of Acerenza's landscape or to gossip with Mark, but to present or suggest some opportunity that he had cultivated.

Mark was eager to hear about it, but he knew he would need to be careful not to be dragged back into the vortex from which he had recently escaped.

CHAPTER 42

Over the next few days, Mark finalized the necessary hires for his wine-making project. Through references he had received from a consultant in the industry, Mark hired experienced people for every key segment of the business. The team he had assembled was impressive. He hired Mauro, a talented and experienced equipment engineer from nearby Bari, to secure an appropriate warehouse with all the necessary state-of-the-art wine-making equipment from Milan and Frankfurt which would crush the grapes and ferment and distill the wine; purchase the appropriate vats for the fermentation process; and obtain the necessary lighting, humidity, and temperature-control equipment for both the temporary and long-term storage of the wine. Mark also hired a plant superintendent who would oversee the conversion of an existing warehouse on the outskirts of Acerenza into a wine-production plant.

And then, of course, Mark needed to have proper marketing, promotion, and sales departments to ensure that all the good work in producing the wine would result in a reasonable return of profit. He hired a marketing director who had worked for a number of years in the central Italian province of Molise and whose contacts included wine purchasers all over the world. And of course, Mark brought a financial controller with a sharp pencil, a keen eye, and his feet glued to the ground on board.

The actual tending of the vineyards, from cultivation to pruning to spraying to harvesting, would be entrusted to Marcello, who had been helping Mark's grandfather at Alvanello for years, and whom had Mark retained to continue in that role since his grandfather's passing. There was no more trusted person, nor a more knowledgeable and experienced vintner in the entire area, than Marcello. Marcello had learned the entire process from his father, who in turn, had learned from his father and so forth, back through the generations. Marcello didn't need lessons on the art of growing the best Zinfandel, Aglianico, and Moscatello anywhere in Basilicata, Puglia, and Campania. The vines were family to Marcello, and were therefore deserving of the same attention as any other member of his family. He was known to treat the vines as if they were his own children, at different times cajoling, scolding, encouraging, threatening, or rewarding them, as circumstances required; neighboring vintners could often hear his every threat, admonishment, or supplication.

Mark had heard the stories about Marcello and had personally confirmed his passion for grapes while observing him at work during harvest time. Mark knew that the most important component of creating a successful brand was safe and secure in the hands of his trusted friend.

Mark had put a good team in place. All were excited to be part of an embryonic project that would oversee the entire process of wine production: from the caring of the vines, to the cultivation of the grapes, to the production of the wine, to the bottling of the wine, and, ultimately, to the marketing of the final product in all four corners of the globe.

The team was thrilled to put Acerenza on the wine-production map, especially because they could always take pride in knowing that they had been involved from the ground floor.

"Santiana-Vino will be the name of our label," announced Mark proudly at a meeting with his newly formed team. He did not explain that the name he had chosen was a derivative of another name, from another time in his life which now seemed so long ago.

CHAPTER 43

Except for a brief visit to Tuscany a few years earlier, John Markham was totally unfamiliar with Italy and Italian customs, especially with the customs of Southern Italy.

What he saw when he and Mark arrived in Acerenza was a corner of the world that time had seemingly left behind. Cars and mules jockeyed for road space—with the mules always winning out. Older men and women were dressed in traditional garb. Gentlemen sported woolen hats, thick flannel shirts, and corduroy pants, while women wore conservative-colored kerchiefs knotted under the chin, blouses that puffed on the shoulder and in the arms, wide ankle-length skirts, and aprons that were worn more for fashion than necessity. For John, it seemed as if he were watching a classic movie. Stores were filled with products that had invariably been made by local artisans. Fresh breads and pastries, baked in brick-lined wood ovens, filled display cases and were still warm to the touch. A camaraderie among the townsfolk created a welcoming and safe environment.

"Mark, this is quite a dramatic change from the helter-skelter activities back in Toronto. It feels like time is irrelevant here, like it's standing still. It's hard to imagine that this is the environment that shaped your early life, given the aggressiveness and ambition that enveloped your career both as a lawyer and CEO."

John had clearly discerned the dichotomy between Mark's early life and the later professional careers he had chosen. "That's why I'm here. I want to come to grips with how I lead the next phase of my life. By coming back to my roots, to how my life began, I felt I could more easily and more objectively identify what I'd been doing, and perhaps be better able to self-analyze my situation and determine how I could continue with my career and find peace within myself."

John absorbed Mark's words and reaffirmed in his mind that his friend had gone through a personal, emotional, and ethical crisis, and that he was coming out of it seemingly reenergized. John had read in fascinating detail all the newspaper accounts describing Mark's departure from Santius. While the speculation was constant fuel in the business literature for weeks, the specific reasons for Mark's departure were never totally uncovered.

"An open and festering control battle between Mark and the Santius board over the direction of the company," was the reason for Mark's resignation, one article claimed, not straying too far from the truth. "A personal feud between Mark and chairman Burton Cavendish," declared another. And so it went. While there was a seed of truth in all these reports, not one ever reported the total story. To their credit, Santius refused to provide any comments on Mark's departure, save to repeat Mark's public statement. By so doing, the speculation soon ended and things at Santius returned to a semblance of normalcy.

The next morning, over a steaming cappuccino at Budini's, John and Mark began their discussion in earnest. John had not come to Acerenza in mid-February for a vacation, as Mark had suspected. He had come to solicit Mark's return home to resume his executive life.

"Your absence has sparked a lot of curiosity among a number of companies. I've received numerous inquiries about you," John said. "You're a hot commodity and people haven't forgotten about your past accomplishments at Santius and in the legal profession," John flattered his friend. "There are 3,500 MBA graduates a year, and every year's crop is brighter, more energetic, and more qualified than the previous year's. With the passage of time, Mark, the inevitable will happen: the hierarchical passing of the baton will occur with each level of candidate stepping up to the higher level. The most talented professionals aim for the most senior executive positions, for which you are currently best suited and for which you should be applying. But you need to reenter the market soon, otherwise, you will quickly become yesterday's news."

John knew that he had hit Mark hard. He also knew, however, that he had given his friend a true message that he could not ignore—at least not if he wanted to get back into the type of position and tenure to which he had become accustomed.

"John, I want to return, but not to a situation where I have to compromise my integrity or ethics. I will never again be involved in an organization where profits or share price become the predominant preoccupations of management or the board." Mark reflected for a moment, as if reliving his experience at Santius during the latter part of his leadership. "A business is successful over the long-term—and I stress *over the long-term*—only if it worries about formulating and implementing strategies designed to benefit the business rather than benefiting those leading it. If that simple rule is followed, everything else falls into place, as it should. The business thrives, personal conflicts are avoided, ethical and reputational compromises are eliminated, integrity is preserved, and, importantly, personal wealth is achieved by its investors. And so, by following that simple script, one gets to the same conclusions that personal greed leads to, but in a way that is honest, unambiguous, and transparent."

John knew that Mark's analysis was sound, but he also knew that this was much easier said than done. "Mark, you have conveniently eliminated personal ambition from your script. Moreover, and you experienced this yourself at Santius, the external pressures imposed by market conditions, market competitors, and hyper-aggressive boards of directors often compel even the most disciplined companies to stray off course. This often can't be helped."

Mark stared at his friend. "That's exactly the point," Mark said. "Those are the usual excuses offered up by unscrupulous management leaders or board chairmen in order to justify misconduct. The reality is that conduct can be directed. Strategies can be adhered to. Personal discipline can be instilled in any organization..." Mark's voice trailed off.

"John, the kind of organization I can see myself leading must possess these characteristics. I would need to be certain that these principles were maintained. I will never again put my personal reputation and integrity on the line for any reason or for anyone—let alone to line the pockets of unscrupulous and greedy parasites. And even then, I am not sure I have the stomach to go through the corporate experience again at this stage of my life."

John was surprised, but not shocked, at Mark's apparent bitterness over the compromises Cavendish had wanted him to accept. On reflection, though, John noticed that while Mark's words were stinging, his tone and demeanor were calm and controlled. John's substantial experience in dealing with the bruised egos of former CEOs told him that Mark's personal emotional bitterness was gone. What was now left was only Mark's fierce determination to be in control in any future tenure.

Mark and John enjoyed the rest of the day as they wandered through the streets of Acerenza. Mark, the proud tour guide, pointed to buildings and sites and gave a brief summary of their historical significance.

Three days later, it was time for John to leave Acerenza, During his short visit, he felt he'd come to understand Mark's personal odyssey. Although he could not fully immerse himself into his friend's inner conflicts, he could certainly see why Acerenza was the perfect venue for reflection and regeneration for Mark. It was normal, John thought, for his friend to go back to his roots to find answers to his personal dilemmas. These were the same roots that had shaped his character.

During the long train ride to Potenza, Napoli, and Rome, where he would catch his flight home, John thought about Mark's recent experiences at Santius and what might be in store for him on his return to Toronto.

As John considered his friend's comments about finding a true measure of balance in his life, the train conductor, with several enthusiastic whistle blows and his right hand in the air, announced with pride, "Siamo arrivati alla bella Napoli. Quindici minuti" (We've arrived at beautiful Naples. Fifteen minutes).

John was famished. It seemed that he had spent considerable energy over the past ninety minutes going over and over Mark's situation. He had found it to be intense, complicated, and tiring, and filled with drama, personal conflict, self-analyses, and soul regeneration.

John hurried off the train, quickly purchased a *cestino* (basket) packed with a *panino imbottito* (filled roll), with a blend of crotonese and Asiago cheeses on the crustiest Italian bun he had ever tasted, a small bottle of wine, and a *Baci cioccolatino* (chocolate kiss) for dessert. *Leave it to the Italians*, mused John. *Even their takeout lunches are fit for gourmands*. Sitting on the train and watching the wondrous early spring scenery whisk by, John devoured his lunch and concluded that this was unquestionably the most delicious cheese sandwich he had ever tasted.

Although Mark had not formally given John the mandate to undertake a search of potential new opportunities for him to consider on his return, nevertheless, John would, out of friendship if for no other reason, see if he could find an appropriate match.

Something at the back of his mind told him this would not be an easy task.

CHAPTER 44

In the Acerenza culture, the vine has always been considered a symbol of the cycle of life. Indeed, the never-ending seasonal cycle of the vine, and particularly its renewal every spring, was somewhat akin to the regeneration of spirit that Mark was currently going through.

Although Mark had always had an appreciation for wine making and the care and hard work it required—which he inherited from his grandfather—he had no clear idea of the technical intricacies involved. As the various members of the Santiana-Vino team discussed the steps in the process, Mark was fascinated by the expertise, knowledge, and background that were essential to the making of a good wine. And when the marketing and promotional disciplines were added, Mark realized that, unlike the folksy romanticism that wine production symbolized, in order to have a successful company, the entire process needed to be carried out like any other business operation.

Needless to say, all these various business components would require financing. Mark needed to employ all his experience and expertise to determine the most effective way to raise capital. The financing component was by far the most complex of the issues he faced, and yet, he felt the most at ease in dealing with it. Years in handling similar financing options allowed him to sift through the various alternatives quickly and surgically. Within three days, and with the input of his controller and his marketing/promotion/sales director, Mark had prepared a pro forma financial statement that he would use to approach the bank at Potenza for the necessary debt financing. He had eliminated equity financing because the last thing he needed at this point was to become involved in a business that he did not fully control. Never again would he allow external influences and pressures guide his conduct, his goals, and the operational results of his business.

And so, the various pieces of the puzzle were put in place. Mark's business strategy could be successfully implemented by the various team leaders he had assembled. With the aid of technology, Mark planned to monitor the progress of every facet of the business from Toronto, save for the four-week period of la vendemmia, when he would, albeit for a short span, again become an Acerenzese.

CHAPTER 45

It was one of those perfect early March Sundays in Southern Italy. The sun's rays had shed their timidity and now shone brightly and warmly. The cathedral's belfry boisterously announced the end of Sunday Mass, as the faithful flock began to descend upon the café patios for midmorning cappuccinos and cornetti. This traditional snack would see the Acerenzese through to the Sunday *pranzo*—the main meal of the day.

The Italian Sunday pranzo is always special. The preparation of *la zuppa* (soup), most often a stracciatella or an egg-drop soup; *il primo* (first dish), invariably a homemade pasta dish; and *il secondo* (main course), normally a chicken, sausage, veal, or pork plate, would usually begin the previous day. There would be little time to accomplish all these time-consuming tasks on Sunday morning, which was reserved for Mass followed by a visit to the café to mingle with friends and discuss the key political or social issues of the day.

Rarely, did an Acerenzese household have the Sunday meal without a circle of close relatives at the table, and if room permitted, one or two close friends.

◆

Little Marco thought of Sunday meals as joyous and fun-loving occasions; he invariably looked forward to them. He especially anxiously waited for dessert, usually a sweet concoction made by his mother or his nonna: cheesecake with homemade sweetened ricotta; almond and pecan clusters held together by honey and melted brown sugar; or *ciambelle* (baked donuts) dipped in hot wine juice.

After these never-ending dinners, the men usually played cards by the fire, their belts loosened to accommodate their happy expanses, while Marco teamed up with his friends to see what innocuous trouble they could generate.

◆

Since his arrival in Acerenza, Mark had often been invited by Luca and, at various other times, by others, to partake in this wonderful ancestral tradition. Since Marina's arrival, they themselves had hosted several of these Sunday pranzi. But not today.

Spring was in the air. It was time to shed winter's remnants and enjoy the beauty of the hills and the valley. Today, Mark and Marina, just the two of them, were having a picnic. They each had a secret: Marina would not tell Mark what she had prepared for their outdoor Sunday meal and Mark would not disclose their destination.

Armed with their food basket and their respective secrets, Mark and his lovely bride headed to their car, hand in hand.

With the car windows rolled down to smell the scented mountain air, Mark drove down the hairpin turns out of town. Mark and Marina passed la Fontana di San Marco, where it was still customary for some of the town elders to hand wash clothes in the huge cement basins which were fed by the fresh mountain water continually spouting from the open mouths of several sculpted lion heads.

Mark proceeded to a side path that was evidenced only by some faint tire marks. A few turns later, he stopped the car. He opened an old wooden gate and accompanied Marina down a rocky path for a few meters. "Just as I remember it," said Mark. "It's as if Father Time decided that this was too beautiful to change and has taken every pre-caution to ensure its endurance."

As the sun shone warmly, Marina looked as if she were a little girl opening gifts on Christmas morning. "It's indescribable. It's the most beautiful sight I've ever seen. Oh, Mark, this is paradise on earth."

A carpet of violets gently swayed in the spring breeze. It was a multicolored cornucopia of the brightest whites, reds, purples, and greens imaginable, as far as the eye could see. It wasn't just the vivid colors of the violets that impressed Marina, it was the scent the flowers generated. The fragrance wafting in the air which, mingled with the perfume emanating from the flowering fruit trees, created a spiritual sensuality that enveloped Marina's mind and penetrated her soul. It was an unforgettable experience that Marina did not want to end.

"I was never a true believer in the healing power of nature," Mark said as he helped his wife empty the picnic basket, "but on a day like this, when we see this virgin beauty, hear the breeze playing soft music with the newly forming leaves and flowers, and experience nature at its finest, I have a sense that I have been missing out on a great natural therapy for much too long."

As Mark sat motionless, transfixed by the beautiful scenery all around him, Marina spread out the feast of his favorite foods she had prepared for their Sunday *pranzo al fresco*. The two long-time lovers sat among the violets, sipping glasses of prosecco and nibbling pieces of Grana Padano and aged Crotonese cheeses as they enjoyed, almost incredulously, the solitude and beauty all around them.

"Mark, you've been so busy, perhaps too busy, working and car-ing for us, that you haven't had the time to do what you're doing now. Maybe you weren't ready to take this step in your life until now," Marina said with her usual, comforting words, "but you've now reached an age, a maturity, when your priorities can change, when you can consider a different path in your life. Whatever you decide to do, I will be right there with you, supporting you all the way."

Their loving embrace signified almost forty years of love and commitment to each other. Theirs was a love that transcended simple physical passion. It was a bond that had been struck at a time when neither of them knew their individual destinies and whether their lives would be permanently intertwined. It was a commitment that had grown stronger over the years and that had formed an inseparable emotional union that would last forever.

Mark thought about his life with Marina and smiled. He was content and satisfied with his marriage. "You've supported me for many years, my love," he said, "and I know I can count on you in the future as we both embark on the next phase of our lives together."

Marina's grip on Mark's arm tightened. She looked at him lovingly and said softly, "Mark, I've always told you that you have an ability to be a good writer. I know you enjoy writing creatively. Would you consider it? Your hard work over the years has thankfully given us financial security. Besides, we don't need much. Dior is as fiercely independent as her dad. She'll continue to seek your advice and counsel, but she'll be just fine on her own. We could scale down, Mark, simplify our life. We don't need a lot of social trappings to be happy." Marina saw a familiar look of pensiveness on her husband's face.

"I know that you'll continue to need external intellectual stimulation and activity in your life, and I'm not suggesting you cut that off, but you might be able to structure a less hectic schedule for yourself and for us, so that we might enjoy experiences like today more often. We could linger with a glass of wine on a restaurant patio or a cappuccino at a café without fretting that our time together might be interfering with an important business schedule that had been preestablished.

"You have nothing further to prove to yourself, to others, or to me. For over thirty years, you have striven for excellence and you have reached the pinnacle of success. You don't need to climb yet another mountain, not after what you've accomplished in life. Maybe it's time to move on to something radically different."

Mark listened intently. *She's right*, he thought. *A change is in my future*. How radical that change needed to be to satisfy his ambition and create a balance in his life was something he still had not yet determined. But he felt he was getting closer to a decision with every discussion with Marina and every mesmerizing interaction with the persuasive and gentle forces of nature.

"The cycle of life renews itself," whispered Mark as he gazed down the valley and up the mountain to the other side. "It is a continuous and never-ending cycle. We are temporary passengers—transients, if you will—on this planet, heading down a fixed and controlled path. We have a say as to which directions, goals, and lives we lead, but the bigger picture is all predetermined for us. Free will and determinism give us the opportunity to show off our individuality, but the bigger picture is controlled by a force that cannot be influenced..."

Mark couldn't help but feel philosophical on a day like this. "We cannot alter man's birth, his maturing physically, mentally, and emotionally, his aging, his death, and perhaps his rebirth. These are the big picture events that are set for us and cannot be changed..." Mark's voice trailed off.

Mark and Marina spent the afternoon chatting and absorbing the beauty around them. As Mark watched the sun begin its daily journey toward the distant mountaintops for its evening rest, Santius, with its material successes and personal conflicts, seemed to be an infinity away. To him, this day had felt like a rebirth, an awakening of his soul.

"It's time to go back," he said to Marina. "The sun drops off pretty quickly behind these mountains, and driving on these twisting roads gets a bit tricky in the dark."

CHAPTER 46

It was a difficult and emotional discussion between the two childhood friends when, in late March, Mark told Luca that he planned to return to Canada in a few days. The venue for that encounter was, expectedly, Budini's Caffè, where all important decisions were normally made by Acerenzesi.

"But Marco, you have settled in and you and Marina have become full members of our community. You're starting the Santiana-Vino business that I'm sure will be a great success and that will bring pride to all your friends in Acerenza," said Luca, pleading with his child-hood friend. "Besides, you look ten years younger. You have no more stress and more peace of mind and time for the important things in life, like time for yourself and Marina, time to enjoy the beauty and peacefulness here, and time to reconnect with your past. Aren't those the important things in life? The things that totally make us happy?"

As Luca continued to remind Mark of all the good reasons he had decided to sojourn in his hometown, and as he recounted all the memories of decades past and described one experience after the other that the two friends had enjoyed, Mark's firm decision to return to Canada seemed somewhat less certain. Luca was a fine advocate, eloquent and persuasive, with flair, drama, and passion imbued in his presentation. With some brief legal training, Mark thought Luca could have had a brilliant professional career as a lawyer.

Nevertheless, even Luca's touching and heartfelt advocacy wasn't enough to alter Mark's fixed plans.

"Luca, your friendship means the world to me. You have reaffirmed my faith in selflessness. I have treasured every minute of our friendship during these five months and nothing has made me happier than to reconnect with you and to tighten our bond once again."

As Mark spoke from the heart, Luca looked to the ground to avoid showing his friend his teary eyes. "My life is now in Canada," Mark said softly. "My roots are here but my parents adopted a new country—a new reality—many years ago. They made sacrifices that have allowed me to fulfill all my career ambitions. My daughter is now following in my footsteps with a promising career of her own. Marina's family is in Toronto. We have our home there and we just can't give that up. It wouldn't be right. It wouldn't be fair," Mark said, as he put his hand on Luca's shoulder.

Luca understood quite clearly that his friend's decision was final. He did not pursue the discussion further.

"But I now have a local business that must be monitored to ensure its success," Mark said with a smile, "and so I will be returning as often as necessary. At least once every autumn, at la vendemmia, I'll be here to enjoy three or four weeks with you and your family. Two of the three Moschettieri will again become active."

Luca's spirits were lifted instantly by the prospect of seeing his friend regularly in the future. But Mark had another important message to convey. "Luca, we have been trusted friends for many years. Although, regrettably, we didn't keep in touch as diligently as we should have, our memories bonded us together, even as we were separately pursuing our lives—"

Luca interrupted him, "*Ma certo*, but of course, my dear friend. Our friendship and love for each other has continued through all these years as if we were neighbors. True friendship and true love don't need the luxury of physical presence. Being near helps, but it is not essential."

Mark discerned a slight smile forming on Luca's lips, and knew that his friend had already determined that this last statement was somewhat discordant with his previous supplication not to leave. Mark could forgive his friend's inconsistency, for love and friendship are not always consistent and straight-lined; they are the nutrients of the heart. They are emotions that can't always be explained or justified, and are often simultaneously inconsistent, oxymoronic, passionate, frivolous, and dramatic. They do have a common theme, though: they form a nucleus of caring, a nexus between two targets that transcends rationalization.

"Luca, I have assembled a very special team of professionals, experienced in all the important facets of the wine-making business. Marcello, of course, will continue to be in charge of Alvanello and look after the vineyard. I have complete faith in his abilities and I trust him totally. But the second phase of this business involves the wine production itself. Not just the making of wine, but also the administrative tasks of keeping accurate records, banking, operations, and marketing and selling."

Luca was now listening intently and Mark felt this was a good sign. "I want you to be Santiana-Vino's general manager, the person in charge of the second phase of the operation. I trust you implicitly, Luca, and I need someone who commands the respect of the Santiana-Vino employees and the whole town. I can't think of a more perfect match for this position. And I want you to have some ownership in the business. I want you to be my partner. I want you to start a new career as the 'big boss' of Santiana-Vino. This way, both Luca Moranni and Marco Gentile will leave behind their past careers and start afresh. What do you say, amico mio?"

Luca's emotions could no longer be contained. He hugged his friend tightly. "You have done me and my family a great honor, my dearest friend. I treasure the trust and faith you have in my ability to help you achieve great things with Santiana-Vino. Of course, it is my great privilege to accept—once we have finalized our negotiations on my ownership stake!"

The close friends laughed and shook hands. Santiana-Vino would, indeed, be placed in the hands of good, trustworthy, and dependable people.

Mark was excited at the prospect of a successful business venture in the place where he had first shaped his ambitions, and where the awakening of his soul had occurred so many years later.

CHAPTER 47

Within a week following their return to Toronto, Marina and Mark reattained a sense of normalcy in their home and daily routines. They had both been busy contacting their friends to announce their return. Mark had had several telephone discussions with John Markham who, it seemed, had been busy formulating a short list of potential opportunities for Mark to pursue. Each such opportunity, Mark knew, would have been thoroughly and flawlessly researched by John. He had targeted several industries and had a strong preference for an environmental company that was on the leading edge of technology for the recycling of waste and converting it to different forms of energy.

"The strategies of these biotechnology companies would be totally synchronized with your own views," John said to Mark one afternoon over the phone. "These entities will become leaders in the new age of environmental preservation and protection, using patented and trademarked technology. Why don't you come and meet me here at the office in three days so that I can show you what I've found?"

Mark agreed to the meeting, before saying good-bye and hanging up. He felt somewhat guilty that his friend had gone through considerable effort to find a corporate niche for him. He was not looking forward to the meeting. He needed to tell John that he had no interest in pursuing any corporate opportunity. He had concluded, after much reflection, that the next phase of his life would take a dramatically different turn; his chosen path would lead him to more personal fulfillment. Mark hoped that John would understand, in the end, that he now sought internal rewards from personally induced gratification, rather than performance judgments measured by compensation subcommittees using corporate earnings ratios.

An executive search counselor would typically be unable to understand Mark's decision. A true friend like John, however, would ultimately accept Mark's decision, and support it.

CHAPTER 48

W elcome home," John greeted Mark.
"It's good to be back."

Over coffee, John described the process he had used to conduct his search, first researching relevant industries and then potential entities within each industry. John described the criteria he had utilized to create a short list of three final candidates. "The purpose of this meeting," John said, "is for you to review these final candidates with me, list them in priority so that I can then approach each of the three search committees, interview them, and determine where your best fit lies."

The process was very analytical and business-like. Very little would be left to chance. The risk of a mismatch would, as a result, be virtually eliminated.

The more Mark listened to John's presentation, the more he knew he had made the right decision in not remaining on the corporate path. Mark knew that no matter how radically different a corporate entity may be, no matter how much it professed ethics and life balances, in the end, what would dictate a leader's behavior would be financial results. Mark knew, perhaps better than anyone, that corporations were simply a legal creation with the sole objective of creating a profit for its investors. Financial performance was, in the end, the only criterion that mattered and that was the principal criterion for reward. Sooner or later, the fine line between legal permissibility and ethical necessity would be blurred. Corporate actions would be initiated or allowed by unscrupulous leaders, or imposed by unscrupulous boards, because they had been ordained as legally allowed—albeit far removed from any acceptable ethical standard.

"John, I have recently decided on my next career direction," Mark stated. John looked at him with curiosity and motioned for him to continue. "I have decided that I don't wish to reenter the corporate arena. I just don't want to play by those rules again. I have no intention of facing the same, or similar, experiences I had at Santius. When I was young and upwardly mobile, I paid little attention to anything except performance and financial results. So long as I had a written legal opinion as to the legality of actions contemplated, and as long as I had a preliminary auditor's opinion that the contemplated transaction was in accordance with generally accepted accounting principles, I took those as a green light to proceed."

Mark stopped for a moment to consider carefully his next statement, and then said, "But as personal reputation, credibility and standing in the community, professional experience, and maturity set in and assume a prominent role in one's life, legal and accounting permissibility are not enough. There must also be ethical and moral standards that stand beside the law or the accounting, and must also be met before a mandate is allowed to proceed."

Mark felt the perspiration forming on his forehead. He knew he was about to slam the door shut to his past. "And these extra-legal standards, especially at this stage of my life, haven't just become preconditions. They have attained such a high level of priority that I don't believe I could ever again assume a corporate leadership role and do justice to the required criteria of creating a return on investment for investors, at any cost."

Mark permitted himself an ironic smile. "Burton Cavendish would almost certainly not agree to a legal strategy that did not put, in the immediate short-term, money in his pocket, even if the strategy was in the best interests of the company and its shareholders in the long-term. What matters to people like Cavendish is a quick and uninterrupted financial fix. It's a personal obsession. This type of attitude is unethical because it is misleading to investors. It is an incomplete strategy because it doesn't consider the long-term devastating effects to be expected. It is improper because it does not disclose that it is largely motivated by a purely-selfish agenda."

The perspiration had now vanished from his brow. Mark felt as if he had just exited a confessional booth.

John knew his friend well. He knew that there was no chance of bringing him around. He knew that, as a friend, what he needed to offer now was his continuing support and friendship. He shook Mark's hand firmly. "What's the verdict, counselor? Is it time to call in the jury?" he quipped.

"Well, the arguments have been made, the evidence is in, and the closing statements settled. Talk to me in five years or so, John, and we'll see what the jury's verdict will be. It will take that long to know," Mark replied, continuing the metaphor.

"For now, I have decided that I want to impart moral and ethical business principles to that segment of the population that can make a difference—students. I first approached Dean Robert Stohlberg at the University of Toronto Law School with my idea several months ago and then again just before getting back from Italy. I have known Bob for years, and, in fact, many years ago I taught an ethics course at the law school. In any event, Bob loved the idea of my proposed teaching project and felt it was high time that the law school offered a course on this topic.

"There is a joint JD and MBA program offered as an adjunct to the JD program. This is the degree program from which the brightest of the bright law school graduates flow and from which the best corporate leaders are chosen. These are the young candidates that need to be influenced so that they will be equipped to handle the Burton Cavendishes of the world...perhaps better than I was able to."

John's expression of incredulity betrayed his otherwise calm exterior. John was stunned by the radical path Mark had chosen. But he respected Mark for putting his principles ahead of material gains and social status. *Mark walks the walk*, John thought.

"Bob has given me carte blanche on the content of the course. I'll mix case law theory with concrete experiences, some personal, to ensure that these bright but impressionable minds understand that this is not simply a theoretical exercise, but a real and evolving reality.

"I'll approach a number of corporate contacts I have and will have the students do confidential case studies on management and boards of directors' decision-making processes."

"When do you start?" John asked with interest.

"I'll set up the course content and materials over the next three or four months and the course will be a second semester course running from January up until the end of the term."

Mark sensed John's next question. "This will also give me time to attend to Santiana-Vino. I plan to be in Acerenza every year for four weeks at grape harvest time to personally monitor the last phase of the grape-gathering and wine-making processes."

Mark paused for a moment. "I no longer want to be a slave to corporate schedules. The combination of teaching and wine making will satisfy my three new objectives. I'll be able to teach corporate ethics, while also having my finger on a small project that, with some care, has the potential to become an interesting financial opportunity. And, most important of all, I'll reconnect with my roots and participate in a more gentle and more simple way of life once a year. This combination will, I hope, give me the balance in life that I've been seeking. And if there is any time left over, I'll attempt to write about what I saw and experienced these last few months—and what I will undoubtedly experience in the future."

John began to respond, but his words were inaudible. Instead, Mark's thoughts wandered back to Acerenza where, toward the end of October, a solitary figure sat motionless, silhouetted against the sky, a witness to the curtain drawing another day to a close. Slowly at first, and then more rapidly, the sun's rays disappeared behind the hilltops, leaving behind a trail of dancing light, mellowing against the approaching darkness.

Soon the sun would set. It would be time for the celestial fireflies to make their nightly rounds while the sun rested and readied itself for its reappearance the next morning.

PART III

Nature's gentle but persuasive
Forces at work.
Transformations begin.
New priorities chosen.
Fresh ambitions
Pervade the mind.
The day's last rays
Dim ancient views.
The day's first light
Introduces future intentions.
And a hopeful start.

CHAPTER 49

In the five years since Mark's return from Italy, he had followed a new path. Mark had found a new balance in his life that allowed for internal, rather than external, rewards. At first, this balance made him a more content person. But that didn't last long.

Mark's passion for action and his ambition to excel had been rechanneled mainly into his three major priorities: his family, Santiana-Vino, and the legal ethics course he taught at the law school. Mark and Marina had never been happier than in the last five years. They spent more time together and their relationship continued to blossom. They discovered that their love had matured into an inseparable friendship that demanded no conditions and required little effort. Mark and Marina were perfectly compatible together, whether in a formal setting, with friends at a game of cards, alone at a café talking about everything or nothing, or just sitting together for long stretches alone in their thoughts.

Mark's executive ambitions, however, had neither disappeared nor been wasted; they had found fertile ground in Dior. Dior had become a senior associate at Merkson LLC, the reputable consulting firm that Mark had retained six years earlier while CEO of Santius. Mark's pride in Dior's achievements was perhaps surpassed only by his wish to counsel her on the potential obstacles and pitfalls that could temporarily detour or stall her drive for excellence. Father and daughter spent innumerable hours discussing issues that were either relevant specifically to Dior's career plans, or generally to the conduct of one's life in the world of business. At every opportunity, Mark imbued Dior with the sense of ethics and morality that had at one time caused his own personal crisis. Like any proud father, Mark vicariously enjoyed living, at least partially, through Dior's youthful career objectives.

The last five years had passed quickly. During that period, Mark often thought back and relived, in his mind's eye, many of his varied life and career experiences. Some of these memories were intense, while others served as a lullaby that transported him into a dream that played out like a movie reel. Mark found that his mental wanderings were often emotional and turbulent. He would on occasion awaken with a start, physically exhausted and drenched in perspiration. Mark did not need any lecture on the power of the mind. He knew from personal experience that the mind is the mandated guardian of the soul, the judge and jury over one's personal conduct, and the sole arbiter in the determination of life's fulfillments or failures. Mark's mind, with all its proven clarity and creativity, was both his most loyal friend and his worst enemy.

Mark alternately felt a deep satisfaction with his life and a tragic deficiency in the attainment of his career and personal objectives. He spent many hours internally debating whether the fulfillment of his ambitions could safely live side-by-side with the nobler objective of realizing personal fulfillment through ethical, but admittedly potentially less effective, conduct. This debate, of course, had no definitive answer. After all, legal standards had been preestablished by society precisely to govern behavior and maintain a uniform standard. Acting within these legal parameters was permissible, society predicated. Acting outside these norms was deemed offensive by society and, therefore, punishable.

One morning, after waking with a start, Mark leaned back into his pillows and thought more about a topic that had often been on his mind: ethics. *Ethics is mainly a non-prescribed notion,* Mark thought, *often varying from person to person, from one society to another. It is largely a subjective, self-imposed rule that one voluntarily adopts in order to achieve personal satisfaction. Why is it not sufficient to guide oneself by simply adhering to established legal parameters? Why isn't legal permissibility a sufficient boundary line to one's actions? Why does one's conduct need both to comply with societal laws and also to some ill-defined, subjective concept that is difficult to judge and reward?*

As Mark pondered these questions, he concluded that the mind was, indeed, a powerful and dangerous weapon that needed to be carefully monitored because, if left unchecked, it had the power to control one's actions and direct them to undesirable destinations.

CHAPTER 50

Mark's winery in Acerenza was thriving. In the first five years of its existence, Santiana-Vino had established itself as an efficient producer and seller of moderately priced wines. Since its second year of existence, it had shown a steady growth in sales and increasing profits.

Mark enjoyed his life as a vintner, even though it was on a part-time basis and, largely, at a distance. Santiana-Vino's investment in technology had allowed Mark to monitor every activity from the comfort of his home office in Toronto. His annual return to Acerenza in October allowed him to participate directly in the traditions of la vendemmia. In his thirty-day stay, he absorbed the sounds and smells of the grape harvest—the very sounds and smells of the life of which he had so long ago been intrinsically a part. The wonders of Acerenza's autumn season provided enough memories to last a year. So entrenched had these experiences become in Mark's senses, so real and concrete, that he played them over and over again in his mind whenever needed—especially in the bleak February days in Toronto. Mark's hyperactive senses had become an escape that allowed him to endure his absences from Acerenza until his next return.

And thus, continued Mark's existence, lodged partly in the concreteness of day-to-day life at home, and partly in the equally concrete reality, thousands of miles away, that he experienced once a year.

Despite its success, Santiana-Vino needed to be reenergized after five years in business. Mark had researched the diversity of products produced in Acerenza and its surrounding areas, and concluded that Santiana-Vino could easily expand beyond wine making, into marketing and selling other food products. Indeed, Mark decided that Santiana-Vino would have a sister company, Santiana-Alimentari, to export Acerenza's oils, cheeses, dried fruits, and preserved vegetables. From the hills and valleys of Basilicata, Santiana-Alimentari would be the conveyor of products nurtured, as they had been for generations, by hard-working and knowledgeable local *contadini* (farmers).

As Mark considered the strategy further, he excitedly decided that he was ready to position Santiana-Alimentari as a global food exporter. Santiana-Alimentari, Mark believed, would put Acerenza on the gastronomic map of the world.

As a result, in a hastily arranged telephone conference, Mark told his Italian colleagues that he would arrive in Acerenza in late March to discuss important strategic updates with them. Sensing their anxiety, he assured them that Santiana-Vino was here to stay and would grow ever stronger in the future.

CHAPTER 51

After his departure from Santius, Mark had not believed it would be possible to give up any of the vestiges of his past power, influence, or prestige. Mark's law practice and executive tenure at Santius had provided the Gentile family with a privileged lifestyle. And so, he and Marina had continued to live in their large mansion in the most fashionable neighborhood in the city—a house that was admittedly too large for the needs of two people—and maintained their country chalet, although they rarely had the time to visit it beyond a sporadic weekend now and then. Mark was also still a member of the golf and country club to which he had belonged for over two decades and had often used as his second office.

The one item he had reluctantly dropped was his Maserati Quattroporte. After much soul-searching, he had concluded that having now come closer to his roots, he no longer felt the need to use his Italian car as the bridge between his past and his current environment. Shortly after Mark's return from Italy, he had purchased the Maserati, partially as an emotional reaction to the Santius situation. Through the perverse logic that often replaces reason and common sense in times of extreme anxiety, Mark had done exactly the reverse of what he had passionately advocated as a Santius executive. But passions were soon replaced by an emotional calm. And, as a result, his 500 horsepower monster had been abandoned in favor of a more docile 250 horsepower hybrid—a car more in keeping with his newly found balance in life.

The continuing question in Mark's mind was whether he and Marina were ready to relinquish these remaining career rewards in favor of a simpler lifestyle. *Would it be possible for us to retrench from the social circles in which we've been so prominent for so many years?* Mark thought.

CHAPTER 52

It was late in the afternoon on February 25, when Professor Mark Gentile left his law school office and began his twenty-minute walk home.

On this bleak and cold February day, the wind whistled and howled without rest. Mark's pace quickened. He was a solitary shadow silhouetted against the white veil of snow. As he turned the corner, he felt the full strength of Mother Nature. The stiff and unrelenting wind stalled his advance and he leaned into the blizzard as he made slow, but methodical, progress, taking one step at a time.

As Mark briefly looked up, the snow and wind seemed to disappear and the scene around him magically transformed into a peaceful spring setting in Acerenza. The end of February marked the end of winter in Southern Italy and the beginning of spring. The hilltops were beginning to awaken from hibernation. The first wild flowers were visible. The trees and shrubs were donning their spring finery of greens, whites, and yellows. A chilly blast, however, brought Mark back to present reality. He felt cold, taken over by a chill that seemed to come not only from the weather around him, but from somewhere inside.

"I need to return to Acerenza at the end of the semester," Mark told Marina that evening. "I think it's time to make some decisions about Santiana-Vino's ongoing strategic plan."

"Oh, I'd love to go back to Italy with you!" Marina said. The two long-time lovers immediately began to plan their trip.

They decided that while Mark briefly attended to the winery, Marina would visit Tuscany.

"I want to explore the beautiful region and reimmerse myself in the culture of the Italian Renaissance," Marina said. Mark would join her in Tuscany once everything was settled in Acerenza.

Mark and Marina shared a love for the Italian Renaissance—*il Rinascimento*, the "rebirth." In their undergraduate years at university, they had spent hours debating Dante Alighieri's various allegories and the metaphorical characteristics of his undying love for Beatrice. When Beatrice died, Marina had mourned Beatrice's death perhaps even more than Dante himself.

And how Marina and Mark had enjoyed those glorious autumn days as students, when, sitting on a bench with coffees in hand, they transported themselves into the sensibilities and imaginary existence depicted by the great Renaissance poet Petrarch. Petrarch prepared Italy for the Rinascimento.

Mark and Marina excitedly planned their itinerary and saw the trip as an opportunity for them to relive their youth together and revive their shared cultural passion.

Mark also saw the trip as an opportunity to reconfirm his own Rinascimento—his own rebirth—through the influences and culture created by the Renaissance scholars several centuries earlier.

CHAPTER 53

Over the next few days, however, an inexplicable melancholy began to invade Mark's mind. The more he attempted to eradicate it, the more pervasive his sadness became.

I'm now in my early sixties, he reasoned. *Dior is successful and I have a loving spouse, financial security, and good health. What more do I need?*

He tried to reassure himself, and yet, there was an emptiness, a void that made him question whether he might have missed something important in life. His anxiety made him uncertain of what direction the next phase in his life should take.

"What now?" he asked Marina, half-rhetorically, while sitting at the dinner table. "Is this how it ends? After years of striving and sacrificing everything to achieve success, do we just confine ourselves to life's plan without further goals and without objectives? Do we become less useful in our environment, precisely at a time when our knowledge and experience should make us most valuable?"

Marina thought of responding, but knew that her husband was on automatic. She understood intuitively that now was not the time to say anything.

Mark's teaching contract with his alma mater was quickly draw-ing to an end. During the past five years, hundreds of students had eagerly taken his legal and business ethics course. Professor Gentile had received dozens of congratulatory messages and testimonials from his students stating that his course had made a difference in their lives. Dean Stohlberg had been eager to renew Mark's contract but Mark had told the dean, months earlier, that he wanted his tenure to end that year, at least temporarily. He had offered to make his course material available to his successor and to assist in any way possible to allow for a seamless transition. He readily accepted the dean's offer to return, on occasion, as a special lecturer to provide his own anecdotes to the class.

Mark felt relieved to end his teaching assignment. Five years of repeating the same moral and ethical message had taken its toll. He had always prided himself in his ability—fine-tuned in his days as a legal advocate—to articulate repetitive ideas with a fresh and creative slant. Nevertheless, on a number of occasions while teaching, he had come to realize that his articulation and creativity had been severely eroded. More and more, he found himself saying the same thing with the same words. Mark's own high expectations of himself were no longer being fulfilled. It was time to move on and accumulate new experiences.

Indeed, the time had arrived for Mark to relinquish his teach-ing duties and embark on a new personal odyssey, though he wondered whether he could actually break away cleanly from his present environment.

CHAPTER 54

As the aircraft ascended to its normal altitude high above Toronto, Mark and Marina saw an expansive blanket of white and gray as far as the eye could see. Although the calendar said the spring equinox had officially arrived, it would be at least five weeks, maybe even longer, before there would be convincing proof in Canada.

The world that awaited them in Italy would be dramatically different, both temporally and meteorologically. Mark was eager, almost impatient, for spring. This season had always marked for him a new beginning. No matter the circumstances in his personal and professional lives, spring unfailingly lifted his spirits and reenergized his soul. This time was no exception. Mark refused to sit back and wait for spring to arrive; he wanted to expedite its arrival.

After landing in Rome, Marina, with her travel books and car and apartment reservations safely tucked away in her travel bag, boarded the train to Florence. There, she would rent a car and head for Fiesole, a small village five miles northeast of Florence. Mark and Marina had spent several weeks in Fiesole as young students. At that time, they traveled on a fixed budget, and decided on Fiesole because accommodations there were substantially cheaper than in nearby Florence. The decision to return to Fiesole had initially been Marina's, but Mark had embraced it as enthusiastically as she had suggested it.

While Marina traveled to Fiesole, Mark headed south to his native town. He felt as if he were indeed traveling to the other side of the world, and about to be reunited with spring.

CHAPTER 55

The serpentine train ride from the capital city of Potenza to Acerenza was a sensory delight for Mark. Human activity was everywhere. Mark observed farmers busy in their fields, plowing the soil and readying it for the spring planting. Horses, cattle, and chickens fed in the green pastures—as they had from time immemorial. Home builders and renovators were either creating anew or sprucing up barns and dwellings. A general awakening from the winter slumber was evident as the citizenry began what would become successive seasons of toil.

Nature also followed a similar path. Everywhere, Mark saw green-shoots of embryonic life—buds later to become dense foliage, shrubs, flowers, and plants. Some were food for the body, others for the soul. All of the plants were in a synergistic balance, all having a primal place in life's order.

The signs and smells of early spring were intoxicating. The air was laden with anticipation and promise. The sun's rays were mellow and amiable. A sense of rebirth was palpable everywhere. *Indeed*, Mark thought, as he looked out the train window, *the human spirit is at its highest at this time of year. Everything is possible. Everyone who is so inclined has the opportunity to become a poet, a singer, a hopeless roman-tic, or a World Series champion. Regrettably though, this sense of inner contentment does not take up permanent residence in the soul. It is short-lived. It soon fades and is transformed into a happy memory to store away until it is retrieved to melt away the January and February chills.*

As Mark observed both man and nature at play, he felt a pervading contentment, as well as an inexplicable anxiety. With this intoxicat-ing scenery all around him, Mark fought hard from slipping into a self-analytical, reflective mood. *There will be time later in Tuscany for reflection*, Mark concluded. For now, there was a business strategy that needed to be reconsidered. Santiana-Vino's affairs would not now allow for further distraction or philosophizing. Important decisions needed to be made.

CHAPTER 56

Upon Mark's arrival, Acerenza itself was a hive of activity; there was a sense of urgency in the air. It seemed as if every man, woman, and child was mobile. At this time of year, the Acerenzesi were at their most efficient. Time was at a premium because the spring season in Basilicata was relatively short lived. By mid-April, the fields needed to be seeded as the growing season started early, and the fruit orchards and vineyards needed to be prepped. Pruning had to be completed before the shoots started growing and budding, and any required spraying and fertilizing needed to be quickly administered. All these tasks had to be squeezed into the abbreviated daylight hours—and while the early spring rains held off. The schedule by which the Acerenzesi abided was not structured by artificial props and clocks, but by nature's more enforceable laws: weather and daylight.

But even during this active season, the gentle townsfolk always found a minute to offer and receive greetings, and to inquire about the health of neighbors' families.

On his arrival, the first face Mark saw was Luca Moranni's. Luca grinned from ear to ear and waved frantically at him from the bus station. Luca embraced his friend as he alighted the bus, grabbed his luggage, and directed him to Budini's Caffè where Amelia Budini was waiting for him with open arms.

"Benvenuto, Marco. Hai fatto un buon viaggio?" (Did you have a good trip?), asked Amelia excitedly.

"Thank you, Amelia. It's good to be back. Yes, I had a good flight over and a relaxing trip from Roma."

Mark was eager to ask Luca about Santiana-Vino, but his friend was adamant that business could wait another day. For now, he wanted to relax and chat about events in Acerenza in Mark's absence, and end the day with dinner at his home.

"We have been working hard preparing a meal of your favorite foods, Marco. You look like you lost weight, no doubt from worrying about business and money. Even in Acerenza, at this time of year, everything is fast paced. Nobody has time to remember the important things in life—those things that truly make us happy and satisfied."

Mark reflected on those words for a moment, and with a quizzical smile, replied, "Everything is relative, my friend."

Amelia emerged from behind the counter with a bottle of Amaro Lucano and three glasses. The three old friends toasted to their health and sat for a long time enjoying one another's company. They were eager to catch up on their respective lives since Mark's departure the previous autumn.

CHAPTER 57

After several days of detailed presentations by Santiana-Vino's marketing, sales, and finance departments, Mark concluded that Santiana-Vino's original strategy, while still sound, needed to be tweaked. Mark presented his new strategy of creating other food brands under the Santiana banner.

"In addition to wine, Santiana will become a recognized name in food importing around the world," Mark announced to Luca and his assembled management team. "Under the name Santiana-Alimentari, we will select, manufacture, package, and export the homegrown products of southern Italy, and Acerenza in particular, to destinations around the world. We'll export olive oil, fruits, herbs, cheeses, and semolina. We'll be known as the door to Basilicata's tastes and smells. We'll bring our foods not only to the millions of Italians abroad, but also to the hundreds of millions around the world who have come to appreciate the tasteful simplicity of our foods and drinks."

Two weeks later, with Santiana's new strategy in place, Luca and his managers began the process of implementation. While Mark traveled, they would update him continuously on its progress. After exchanging salutations with Luca, Amelia, and the Santiana team, Mark embarked on the trip north to Florence to meet Marina.

Marina, it seemed, had so immersed herself in her research and studies that she felt and acted like she had as a student, forty years earlier. She was flirting with the idea of becoming a full-time student in Renaissance literature at the local university. Her mind had become preoccupied with the world of literature, full of ethereal reality, philosophy, and allegories. Over the last two weeks, Mark and Marina had discussed their respective activities through daily telephone calls. With every discussion, Mark had sensed that his lovely bride had crossed the magic threshold from interested reader to protagonist—a crossing that, as students, they had both believed was essential in order to engage in a critical dialogue with an author or poet.

The train ride from Acerenza to Potenza, Naples, and eventually Rome was tortuous and exhausting. At Stazione Termini, Mark purchased a lunch basket of Italian delicacies and boarded the *direttissimo* (fast train) to Florence.

Mark sat by the window, his back to his destination, and ate his lunch. After finishing his meal, he relaxed with a glass of wine. The speeding train created the sensation that he was accelerating toward the future while looking back at the past—and leaving it behind. In reviewing his accomplishments to that point, Mark concluded that his business ambitions had been fulfilled. He had engaged in a successful legal career and a rewarding executive tenure. True, he had not seen his Santius strategy deployed, but his departure was not so much out of failure as it was out of wanting to ensure that his ethics and morality were not eroded by personal agendas and financial greed. He had cut short his tenure at Santius voluntarily and with good reason. Unlike Cavendish, Mark would never allow a personal financial agenda to obfuscate the need to do what was right.

The train's arrival in Siena shook Mark out of his trance. Dozens of outgoing and incoming passengers hurried before the train announced its departure for Florence. Siena was located at the heart of Central Tuscany and its main rival for centuries had been Florence.

Beginning at the end of the thirteenth century, the two cities were the two most influential cities in Europe. They were home to the European Renaissance, a period of such profound cultural and ideological change that it transformed all of Europe after the Dark Ages.

As the train moved toward Florence, Mark's own philosophical voyage also continued. *What can I do to fulfill my remaining ambitions? Is there anything left to achieve?* These were the questions and themes that Mark and Marina, as young students, had sought to uncover. These were the humanistic issues that the Renaissance scholars had advanced. These were the ideals that had lifted Europe into a transition from the Middle Ages to the Rinascimento. These were now the lofty answers that Mark was seeking and that, he hoped, would put his soul at peace.

In less than one hour, Mark thought sleepily, he would be reunited with Marina.

CHAPTER 58

Marina had settled in well in Tuscany. She had rented a furnished apartment on Via di San Francesco in Fiesole. The apartment was small but charming and was furnished with antiquities—some of them going back to the Etruscan era, according to the exaggerated claims of the affable landlord Signora Teresa. From the balcony, one could see Fiesole spread out past the public gardens and onto the foothills of the Mugello region. On a clear day, from the top of Fiesole's surrounding hilltops, Florence and its surrounding countryside were quite visible, many miles to the southwest.

Fiesole had been well known to Mark and Marina during their student days. They had last visited it in the early 1970s when they were studying Etruscan and Roman influences on the peninsula.

"Mark, nothing has changed here in almost four decades," Marina excitedly told her husband when she met him at the train station. "It is such a wonderful experience seeing people preserve older buildings rather than raze them to the ground for some condominium building or shopping plaza. Here, every structure is exactly as we remember it."

Mark detected a youthful enthusiasm in his wife that he remembered well from their student days. It was an infectious attitude that immediately transformed Mark into a scholar of philosophy and literature—the two disciplines he had reluctantly relinquished in favor of pursuing a career in law. But he had never lost his love for the arts and, indeed, had tried whenever possible to reenter the world of the metaphysical, of literature and philosophy. In the last five years, since his departure from Santius and his arrival in Acerenza, Mark had begun to reestablish a deep connection to his roots and, with it, a rebirth of emotions and preferences based on the loftier ideals with which scholars had been grappling for centuries.

"Let's go for a walk around town so that you can get reacquainted with Fiesole," Marina said. "You've been sitting on a train for hours. The walk will do you good. We'll work up a good appetite, and then, for dinner, I have a surprise for you."

As they toured Fiesole, Mark recognized many of the sights and structures he had known so well forty years earlier. From the Duomo di San Romolo, they walked through Piazza del Mercato and on toward the Teatro Romano, the ancient amphitheatre that had been built in the first century B.C. and was still used every summer for Estate Fiesolana, the festival of music, dance, arts, and drama. Mark recalled that he and Marina had seen a dramatic play in the Teatro on a balmy July evening many years back. As he stared at the empty giant structure, Mark remembered how blissful and carefree that evening had been, and how fortunate they had felt to be sitting on stone seating that had been constructed by man, without the aid of technology, over two thousand years earlier.

As they neared the end of their walking tour, the Tuscan sun began to set. Mark gazed over the nearby hills and was mesmerized by the mellowness of the light, the sun half hiding behind the rows of cypress trees dotting the landscape. For centuries, poets had been attempting to capture, always unsuccessfully, these wondrous scenes all across the Tuscan countryside. Mark, struck by this beauty all around them, whispered, "Man, no matter how talented, can never match the hand of nature." And as if to punctuate that comment, the sky turned into a canvas of gold, blue, and pomegranate, and the sun offered its last good-byes. A chorus of cicadas triumphantly announced the end of another day.

Marina, sensing that her husband had slipped away from the present, gently tightened her grip on his hand and guided him toward a narrow cobblestone path that would lead them to their dinner destination.

CHAPTER 59

Remo's Cucina Nostrana had been offering home-cooked Tuscan specialties for decades. The small trattoria had become a legend in the area and patrons would regularly come from as far away as Empoli and Prato to dine on Remo's simple but tasty concoctions.

That evening, as usual, the place was full except for one table in the far corner, beside the fireplace. The moment they entered the trattoria, the smells and sounds magically transported Mark back to their student days, when traveling across Europe on a budget of five dollars a day meant they could only afford to eat the simplest foods and sleep in the most basic accommodations. Mark fondly recalled Remo's and quite vividly remembered the affable Remo who, sensing that Mark and Marina's appetite was bigger than their wallet, had offered them a feast that, even now, Mark's taste buds could not justly describe.

Without assistance or prompting, Marina led her husband to their table in the corner, where a carafe of local Chianti had been awaiting their arrival. Within a few minutes, Remo emerged from the kitchen and stood by their table, smiling and seemingly bigger than life. Mark offered Remo his hand.

"You look the same as you did four decades ago," Mark lied. Remo enjoyed his exaggeration. In Italy, there was an almost indecipherable line between a slight exaggeration and outright untruth when it came to one's physical appearance.

Remo grabbed Mark by the shoulders, hoisted him out of his chair, and hugged him tightly. "Benvenuto, Marco. Ben tornato" (Welcome back), he said loudly, as Marina joyfully witnessed their reunion. Over a glass of prosecco, Mark, Marina, and Remo quickly recounted their first meeting over forty years earlier. After a few minutes, duty called and Remo hurried away to create his usual magic in the kitchen.

Marina had planned the evening perfectly: no menus, no specials of the day, and no servers. The meal was exactly what they had eaten many years earlier on that fateful evening. The only difference was dessert.

Tuscan cuisine represents gastronomy at its most sophisticated, but is derived from humble and simple cookery. It is food that is basic and disarming. Its genius lies in the simplicity of its preparation and the freshness of its ingredients. That evening, as it had many years earlier, their meal began with the famous Tuscan *crostini al vinsanto*—small slices of toasted bread dipped into *vinsanto* (Tuscan dessert wine), topped with a finely ground cooked sausage, and finished with rosemary and other seasonings. Their second appetizer was *fiori di zucca fritti* (fried pumpkin flowers), which were dipped in an egg and flour batter and fried until golden brown.

Their main dish followed. *Pappa al pomodoro* (tomato bread soup) was served with *pappardelle e anatra* (strips of pasta with a duck sauce), a dish cooked perfectly al dente. The dishes were so fresh and aromatic that Mark and Marina could taste each individual ingredient: fresh field tomatoes, thyme, celery, and onions. Each instrument collectively merged into an orchestral symphony of taste that tickled the taste buds.

For dessert, Remo offered his daily special. That night it was *zuppa inglese alla fiorentina*, a delicious local trifle brushed with marsala.

Mark and Marina enjoyed the meal. It was unforgettable both for its indescribable taste and because it represented their adventurous and carefree times of yesteryear.

"Food in Italy is, in itself, a sufficient reason to move to the peninsula," Mark said, only half joking. Marina agreed.

After several hours of eating, laughing, and talking, they told Remo they would be back very soon and set out for the short walk back to their apartment. They didn't exchange a word; their strong grip on one other's hand was all the communication they needed. They both felt happy, secure in their relationship, and excited about their future life as one.

Mark suddenly stopped in the middle of the street, and as the Tuscan moonlight shone on Marina's face, he kissed his wife lovingly. He felt that they had so much in common, had shared so much of themselves with each other for so long, and had formed an intrinsic and indivisible union. They continued on silently toward their apartment. During that unforgettable evening in Fiesole, they needed no words to describe their personal contentment.

CHAPTER 60

Mark and Marina had been in Tuscany for two weeks. While their home base was Fiesole, they traveled daily to other parts of the province. Florence, of course, was their most frequent destination, but they also took daily trips to Perugia to the south, and Pisa and Livorno to the west.

They spent glorious days exploring markets and antique stores and traveling around the countryside. Every café they encountered became a special destination. Often, they would engage in thoughtful conversations that would last hours; the issues that interested Mark and Marina were not easily solved. These same matters had preoccupied philosophers and humanists for centuries, without drawing answers.

One late afternoon, as they were returning from a day trip to Siena, Mark and Marina stopped for drinks in the small hilltop village of Panzano in Chianti, an area, as the name suggests, in the heart of the Chianti region. High up and overlooking the valley below, Panzano in Chianti offered breathtaking views from every side. There were vineyards as far as the eye could see and fruit orchards interspersed in a pastoral setting that was pure yesteryear. Little had changed from the days when the Etruscans had ruled the area.

On the patio overlooking the steep valley, the two Tuscan adventurers sat staring at the beauty all around them. It was the perfect spot for reflection. Only occasionally did they remember to sip on their vinsanto and nibble on their *biscotti di Prato*.

"I've been thinking that the most important thing in life is to live it to one's full potential," Mark said.

"I agree," Marina said. "We must awaken our senses and our sensibilities as much as we can. We need to appreciate not simply the intricacies of modern technology, but also life's wonderful simplicities, like the wonder of a beautiful sunset, the beauty of a carpet of freshly fallen snow, the feel of walking barefoot on a field of freshly cut grass, and the rituals of nature every spring and autumn."

Mark had often considered whether the next phase of his life would be a continuation, more or less, of the life and lifestyle to which he had become accustomed, or whether it was time for him and Marina to break away and ignore the societal pressures imposed on them and live the life they really wanted to lead.

"We've both had very fulfilling careers and our daughter is an exceptionally talented and loving young woman, mostly because of your efforts," Mark said to his wife as he lovingly gazed into her eyes. "We've led such busy lives and it's difficult to slow down and switch priorities now. We're so accustomed to working for external rewards that it feels odd to be satisfied only with personal fulfillment. Yet, that's the only true reward that lasts in the long-term.

"I have found, in the last few years, that accepting who I am and being happy about it are the only objectives I need in order to find satisfaction and happiness."

"Well, let's do something about this. We're healthy, we have all our faculties intact, and we're still young enough to appreciate all this..." Marina's hand extended toward the valleys and the adjoining hilltops. "I think it's time to radically change our life priorities. We have roots in Italy, and Santiana-Vino is doing well. We could be happy living in

Italy, Mark, and it's obvious that you have a very deep connection to your country of birth."

Mark sat silently, glass in hand, staring out at the hills as that famous Tuscan sun was about to set behind the Chianti Mountains.

"Dior is a bright, energetic, and independent woman. She'll be fine without us across town. Besides, our taking up residence in Italy will give both us and Dior a chance to visit each other frequently. We could live in Acerenza during the grape harvest and have an apartment in Tuscany or Sorrento or the Amalfi coast. Let's do it, Mark. Let's cut our umbilical cord to the past."

Mark listened carefully and sat silently for a long time. A smile formed on his lips as he looked down from the hilltop and imagined a small boy running recklessly down the hill toward the valley, deftly twisting and turning around trees and other obstacles, never losing speed. Mark could almost hear the screeching of steel wheels grinding against train tracks as the youngster, now reenergized, picked up his pace and sprinted into the open arms of a familiar elderly man standing at the finish line, moments before the shrill of a whistle, reverberating in the valley, announced that the train had once again finished the race in second place.

It was during those magic moments, as they both became lost in the beauty all around them, that Marina knew Mark had finally found Marco.

The visitor
Seeks permanence.
The distant land
Of initial refuge
Embraces and comforts.
A peaceful coexistence
Between idealism and ambition
Is struck.
The mind is at peace.
The soul ceases its
Wandering journey.

ACKNOWLEDGMENTS

Writing fiction is a terrific experience for an author. He is able to use a lot of imagination and a little creativity to exaggerate, understate, and embellish almost any person, action, description, activity, or even reality. A dream can be turned real and an event can be concretized at will, with the flick of a pen.

There is an Acerenza, a picturesque mountaintop town in the province of Basilicata in south central Italy, from which I drew my inspiration. However, there is no Luca Moranni nor Gianni, Amelia, Father Caius, Marcello, Dean Robert Stohlberg, John Markham, nor Burton Cavendish except as real characters in my fertile imagination. These characters, though, do emanate from individual and unrelated experiences, or perhaps dreams, I may have had, consciously or unconsciously, in my daily existence.

There is no Dior, and there is no Marina. But I do have a loving wife, Anita, and a wonderful son, Richard. It is to them, and for their continuing support and love, that I dedicate *Finding Marco.*